Youngin'

Arlene Brathwaite

Library of Congress Number: 2005909476

ISBN: 1-57087-699-1

This book was printed in the United States of America.

To order additional copies of this book, contact:

Variety A+
PO Box 3807
Albany, NY 12203
(518) 729-4569
www.arlenebrathwaite.com

Foreword

YOUNGIN is a crazy street fiction novel that delivers intrigue in the form of drama, drugs, relationships and more drama. Money, money, and mo' money is the motto of the lead character, Brian Moore. Due to his chosen lifestyle, Brian matures quickly, far beyond his young 18 years of age.

Caught up in the fast life with his friends, Devon and Jason, Brian lives life on the edge. In some ways, such as establishing his reputation, he is a savvy businessman. By conducting his street business and building his reputation, although he is young, Brian becomes a contender in the larger interworkings of the street business. Will he be able to sustain his reputation and not catch a case with the law?

On the other hand, he is just a kid who still lives at home with his parents and has made the wrong decisions. Although Sonia is a good girl to have by his side because she is good to him and good for him, Brian continues to step out of his relationship with not one but several ladies. Will his promiscuous ways catch up with him and cost him Sonia's love?

What plays out on the pages of YOUNGIN is anyone's guess. At first, I thought it was somewhat of a typical read, but there are unexpected plot twists, which engages the reader. Written in the third person, author Arlene Brathwaite has penned a street novel that seems all too realistic. She incorporates a bevy of various characters to create subplots to roll along with the overall drama of the story. If you're a fan of street fiction, YOUNGIN is not to be overlooked.

Reviewed by Nedine Hunter
of The RAWSISTAZ™ Reviewers

Coming Soon
Also by Arlene Brathwaite

Ol'Timer
Soul Dancing
I'll Take You There

Brian Moore is suffering a mid-life crisis at the age of eighteen. His life revolves around getting money. For him, that means armed robberies and stick-ups. He has baby mama and baby mama family drama. The only thing stable in his life is his fiancée, Sonia. She's a college student with a relentless passion to make it out of the hood with or without Brian. For the first time in his life, Brian can't straddle the fence. He has to make a decision. Will he be loyal to the streets which raised him and made him who he is today? Or will he be loyal to a girl who is promising him a better tomorrow?

Acknowledgments

God is the greatest. He has given me the strength and resolve to turn my life's upsets into assets. Although I've made terrible judgments because of the life I chose to live, I refuse to let my past haunt my future.

To my people on the grind, times are hard, but we're harder. Put faith in your potential and then just watch the possibilities unfold before your eyes.

I owe that lesson to my family and friends who, at one time, put more faith in me than I did.

To my better half Chris Brathwaite for putting up with me for fourteen plus years, you are my inspiration, my soul mate for life.

My daughter Tamicka Ramey for always being there for me, you are my right hand.

My son Sherodd Craft for the poetry you write. Your words have been a great inspiration to me.

My daughter Marshay Brathwaite for being there when I needed you the most.

My grandchildren Jah'Kyra, Ja'Quah, and Keyaj'rah for always keeping a smile on my face, I love you all.

My extended family, Melissa, Quesha, Sasha, and Daytwaun, my life has been touched by your presence.

My family and friends who are too many to name, thank you for your continued support.

Chapter 1

"Yo, he's pulling up," Jason spoke into his head-piece connected to his cell phone.

Brian put his cigarette out and casually watched the smoke grey Lincoln Navigator pull up in front of the brownstone.

Jason, who was parked directly across the street, watched the 6' 2", 250-pound black man step out of the truck.

Big man looked up and down the dark street, like he was expecting someone to jump out of the shadows and rob him. The only person he saw was a young man sitting on the brownstone steps, wearing a Yankee baseball cap, talking on his cell phone. As he stepped away from his truck, he stopped in his tracks. He spotted Jason sitting in the black Lexus SUV.

Jason pretended not to notice him as he fiddled with the radio. His eyes widened when the man reached into his truck and pulled out a leather pouch. He unzipped it and slipped it in his trench.

"He's strapped, y'all," Jason said into his head-piece.

Brian's heart was pounding so hard between his ears that he couldn't hear Jason trying to talk him out of the robbery.

All Brian focused on was the 20Gs he knew the man was wearing around his waist.

The man climbed the brownstone steps heading straight for him. Brian casually pulled the cigarette from the back of his ear and lit it, while nodding to the man.

He nodded back and kept moving.

When the man got to the top of the stairs, Brian reached in his coat pocket and grabbed the butt of his Beretta 9mm. Instantly, he felt a surge of courage shoot through his veins. His chest expanded, his nose flared, and his gonads grew to the size of basketballs.

The man pressed the top button on the intercom.

"Who dat?" said the voice through the intercom.

"It's me."

Brian spun around and ran up the steps two at a time when he heard him being buzzed in. He was right up on him when a scream pierced the night.

"Henry, look out!" the woman yelled from the passenger side of the Lincoln Navigator.

The man turned around stunned to see the Yankee-capped teen pointing a gun at him. Out of sheer fright, he shoved Brian and ran toward the entrance.

Brian lost his footing and slid down several steps before regaining his balance and running back toward the man.

As the man swung the door open, a gloved fist smashed him in the face, knocking him on his butt. Through teary eyes, he saw another Yankee cap-wearing teen cocking back his fist to hit him again. Still dazed, he covered up as the assailant threw a flurry of punches to his face and head.

Brian reached the top of the steps and kicked the man in the kidneys. The man grunted in pain.

Two bullets ricocheted off the steps, taking Brian and his partner Devon by surprise.

"What the fuck," Brian said just before ducking two more shots that came from the Lincoln.

The woman opened the passenger side door screaming her boyfriend's name as she took aim at Brian.

Before she could squeeze off another two shots, a hail of bullets riddled the Navigator and penetrated her back.

"Come on!" Jason yelled, pulling the Heckler and Koch submachine gun back inside the truck.

When the man saw his woman face down on the sidewalk twitching, he went berserk.

"You motherfuckers!" He grabbed Brian by the front of his pants and started swinging with his free hand, grazing Brian's cheek, chin, and jaw.

Shocked at the big guy's speed, Brian aimed at the man's chest and squeezed the trigger. The man's whole body went rigid as Brian squeezed the trigger again and again.

The horrified look on the man's face rooted Brian to the ground. The man's lips moved, but all Brian could hear was him choking on his own blood. Brian went numb.

What did I just do? he thought to himself. He watched the man slide down the steps. The thump of flesh and bone bouncing off the concrete steps made Brian's skin crawl.

Devon tapped him on the shoulder. "We got to go, Bee."

They jetted down the steps. When they got to the bottom, Brian opened the man's coat and ripped off the money belt. As they both ran to the jeep, Brian felt raindrops hitting his face. He knew then that he would never be forgiven because God was crying.

Chapter 2

As they turned on to the highway, Brian kicked Jason's seat. "What the fuck happened back there?"

"I didn't see her."

"How the fuck you didn't see her? She was sitting right in the passenger's seat."

"Yo, Bee. I swear, I didn't see her."

"Three years, Jay. Since the age of fifteen, we've been doing this and never had to fire a single shot."

Jason looked at Brian through the rearview mirror. "I fucked up, Bee."

"You more than fucked up."

Brian sat back, eyeing the money belt. "You all right, Dev?"

"I'm cool, Bee."

Devon was always cool. He could be in front of a firing squad, and if you asked him how he was doing, he would say, "Everything's cool."

"So what now?" Jason asked.

"We head back to Queens and lay low."

"What about Bret?" Devon asked.

"Don't worry about him," Brian said, "I know how to handle him."

Brian opened the money belt and counted the hundred-dollar bills. "It's all here," he said. "Just like Bret said it would be." He counted off three thousand and gave it to Devon.

"Cool," Devon said accepting the cash.

Brian counted off two thousand and shoved it in Jason's coat pocket. He waited for him to inquire about the other thousand so he could curse him out for putting their lives in jeopardy.

Jay knew he fucked up, so he didn't dare ask.

Brian pocketed five thousand and put Bret's ten thousand in his other pocket.

Ten minutes later, they pulled up behind the Mobile Gas Station where they parked their cars. Devon was the first to get out.

"I'm out of here," he said walking toward his car. "See y'all later."

Brian nodded. "No doubt."

"Wipe this bitch down good," Brian said to Jay, referring to the stolen Lexus. He wiped the Beretta down and handed it to Jay. "And get rid of this."

"Don't worry, Bee. I got this."

Brian stared at him for a moment before hopping into his Nissan Pathfinder and pulling off.

Chapter 3

Brian crept into the house at a quarter to midnight. He was surprised his mother wasn't up waiting for him. He looked into the microwave and grabbed the plate of food she left for him and headed upstairs to his room.

As he undressed and got into the shower, he replayed the whole scene in his head. He never planned on shooting anyone much less killing them. He took pride in running up into crack spots, number holes, or where ever else Bret sent him and rob the joint without having to shoot anyone. But now, he had a man's blood on his conscience, and it made him want to throw up.

He toweled off and dialed Sonia's number. She picked up on the fourth ring.

"Hello?"

"Damn, baby. You were sleep?"

There was a pause. He could imagine her putting on her glasses to look at the clock.

"It's 12:30 in the morning, Brian."

"And?"

"And? Why you calling so late?"

"I just wanted to see what you were doing."

"What do you think I would be doing at 12:30 in the morning?" Brian didn't answer.

She sucked her teeth. "You just getting in?"

"Yeah."

"Where were you?"

"Out with Devon and Jason."

She paused. This time, he could see her sitting up, getting ready to give him the business.

"I don't know why you hang out with them crab-ass niggas. All they do is get you in trouble."

"Baby, you know it ain't like that."

"The three of you jump a dude at Green Acres Mall, and who's the only one to get arrested for it?"

"Baby, the only reason why I got arrested—"

"Fuck why you got arrested. Who had to come bail you out because your crab-ass friends couldn't come up with a measly five hundred dollars?"

"You taking this some place else."

"And when you copped out to that gun charge because you didn't want to snitch Devon out, who came to Riker's Island every weekend faithfully for eight months to see your black ass and jerk you off in the visiting room?"

"Listen, I didn't call to argue with you. I just needed to talk to you." Sonia could hear the uneasiness in his voice. "Why, what happened?" He needed to talk about tonight. He needed her to say that everything was going to be all right, but he knew that was only wishful thinking.

"Nothing happened. I just wanted to hear your voice before I went to bed. I'm gonna give you a call tomorrow, love you."

Sonia paused before answering. "I love you, too."

Brian hung up and stared at the ceiling.

Chapter 4

Brian stood on the corner of Merrick and 230th street when Bret pulled up in his milk white Ford Explorer. Brian called him earlier that morning so he could give him his cut of the money.

Bret lowered the passenger side window. "Hop in, nigga." Brian climbed in and couldn't help but stare at him.

"What are you looking at?" Bret said.

"Nah, I'm just looking at you and remembering you back in PS 30 when motherfuckers used to take your lunch money and give you wedgies."

"And all them motherfuckers are either dead or sucking dick to buy my crack. Speaking of which, everything went smooth last night?"

Brian pulled out the 10Gs and threw it in the glove compartment.

"There was a little problem."

"What's that?"

"Shit got hectic. He had a chick in the truck with him. We didn't see her 'til it was too late. She screamed, put him on point. He reached, I reached..."

"And?"

"And I shot him."

Bret let out a loud sigh. "Is he dead?"

"Yeah, and the chick too."

Bret's head whipped toward him. "You killed the bitch too?"

"She was shooting at me. It was either her or me."

Bret shrugged his shoulders. "Fuck it, shit happens. One less nigga to compete with, and one less bitch to worry about."

Bret turned on to the Eastern Parkway. "I'm gonna need you to do me a favor."

Bret never asked for favors. He hated to have them hanging over his head.

Brian fumbled with the radio. "Oh, yeah, what's that?"

"I hooked up with some cats a few weeks back at a beach party in Long Island, and they plugged me into a gold mine."

"A gold mine?"

"I dropped my workers off at their spot in LI, and they made 5Gs in three hours."

"Get the fuck out of here."

"My boys told me that the fiends were coming out of the woodwork. They were dropping out of trees, crawling from under cars, and shit like that."

They both laughed at the exaggeration.

"So what's the favor?"

"I can easily clear ten Gs every weekend if I had somebody out there I could depend on to handle that amount of product."

"So you trust me now?" Brian said with a smug smile.

"I said somebody I can depend on, nigga, not trust. I don't even trust my own sister."

Ah Trish, Brian thought. *Trish with the bubble booty and the juicy lips. Damn! Her pussy tasted like cotton candy, and she'll suck a niggs's balls through his dick if he let her. It's always the innocent-looking ones.*

"Okay, so when we gonna work this out?"

"Right now, nigga, where you think we headed?"

Chapter 5

Twenty minutes later, they pulled up in front of a bodega. Brian made a mental note of the directions on how they got there.

Ever since they got off the expressway, the scenery was eating at him. Everything looked perfect, too perfect. All the houses looked the same. There were no projects, no cracks in the sidewalks, and the streets were squeaky clean. The town looked like a Hollywood scene from the movie *Utopia*.

Bret shut the truck off and leaned back in his seat. "So what do you think?"

"Think about what?"

"The spot."

He had to be joking, Brian thought, but when he looked over at him and saw that he was dead serious, he started to laugh.

"What you laughing at?"

"This is the spot? Who you selling to? Casper?"

Brian looked at the store fronts: a bodega, a strip bar, and a church. "Is that a real church?"

"That's what I said when I first got out here, Bee."

Brian shook his head. "How can someone keep a church open in the middle of heavy drug traffic?" This was definitely an episode for the *Twilight Zone.*

"Let's do this," Bret said, jumping out his truck. "They should be in the bar."

Brian hopped out the truck and scoped out the area, trying to imagine how these cats were making thousands of dollars in a single night.

As they reached the door, it swung open and in front of them stood the smallest, biggest dude Brian ever saw. He was about five feet four inches and packed with muscle. There was no doubt in Brian's mind what this cat did on his bids upstate.

He smiled at Bret and blinded Brian with his gold teeth. "Peace, god," he said stretching out his hand to Bret.

Bret gave him a pound and put his arm around his shoulder. "Yo, Powerful, this is my man, Bee."

The beast sized him up. His nose flared like he was trying to identify his scent. "What up, Bee?"

Brian put on his meanest ice grille. "What up?"

Powerful turned his attention back to Bret. "The gods are in the back."

As they walked to the back of the bar, Brian spotted only one patron in the bar. He was getting a lap dance by the ugliest stripper he had ever seen. She was bucktoothed with stringy hair. And the stretch marks all over her body made her look like a human road map. He turned his attention toward the dudes they were approaching. All of them were checking Brian out as he walked up. They all wore tank tops, which highlighted their ridiculously huge muscles and their jailhouse tattoos.

Bret slapped them all five.

After going through the peace god this and peace god that, he introduced Brian. "This is my man, Bee."

The three of them nodded.

"Bee, this is Equality, Knowledge, and I—God."

They exchanged superficial handshakes and smiles.

"He's going to be regulating for me," Bret said.

"What happened to the other two?" Powerful inquired.

"They'll be working the other end, bagging up and shit like that. Besides, you said you didn't like them anyway. You said they were knuckleheads."

Powerful smiled. "I'm surprised they didn't shit their pants when we had that run-in with Robocop last weekend."

"Robocop?" Brian asked.

"Yeah," Equality jumped in. "He stay trying to bust somebody. He rolled up on them last weekend and made them strip right there on the corner. He smacked them up, took their money, and told them that he was going to put a bullet in their asses the next time he saw them up around here."

If Equality was trying to intimidate Brian, it was working.

For the next hour, they shared their war stories and backyard chases they had with Robocop. Although each one of them said that they would put a bullet in him if they had the chance, Brian could hear the terror in their voices.

On their way back to Queens, Brian struggled to see his future, but like a lot of ghetto teens, he was nearsighted.

He couldn't see past his twenty-first birthday. He could see Sonia graduating from college and being a lawyer like she always wanted. He envied her because she had their lives all mapped out for them— a life that he was too afraid to tell her that he couldn't see.

Chapter 6

Bret dropped Brian off at Andrea's house. "If Sonia ever found out about you and Andrea, she would cut your dick off and stick it up your ass."

"Sounds like jealousy to me," Brian retorted.

"Fuck you, Bee."

Brian threw up the peace sign as Bret drove off.

Andrea came bursting out the house before Brian got a chance to ring the bell.

"Hi, Daddy," She ran into his arms and kissed him long and hard. He palmed her butt and grinded his crotch against hers.

She turned around and parked her plumped-ass smack on his growing johnson. "I missed you, Daddy," she said looking over her shoulder at him.

He kissed her neck. "I missed you too, Ma. You home alone?"

She swayed her butt back and forth on his now rock-hard johnson. "Why? You want to give me some of that?"

Without a word, he walked her inside and shut the door. They never made it to her bedroom. They would always wind up on the living room couch, dining room chair, or the staircase.

Andrea wasn't the type Brian could fuck on a bed, missionary style. She performed best when he treated her like a hoe. He made her strip seductively and play with herself. He held out for a whole two minutes before grabbing a handful of her hair and bending her over the couch. She loved it doggie style, and she couldn't cum if he didn't rough her up a little.

Seeing her ass jingle as he plowed into her was too much for him.

"Spread you ass cheeks, baby, I'm cumming."

Andrea reached back and opened wide.

Brian pulled out and shot his load right between her crack.

Andrea spread her ass cheeks wider as Brian rubbed the head of his dick on her butt cheeks. "Oh, Daddy, that feels so good."

With one thrust, he sank his dick back into her.

Andrea arched her back and pushed back on him until she felt his balls smacking against her. She groaned as she bit down on her lower lip.

Brian reached around and pinched her nipples while she played with herself.

She's a fucking animal, Brian thought to himself. *Sonia would never let him do this to her.*

"I'm cumming, Daddy, I'm cumming."

Andrea bucked harder, trying to get every centi-meter of Brian's dick into her. As she came, her walls spasmed around his dick, and he found himself cumming again right along with her.

Chapter 7

Brian laid limp in the bathtub as Andrea bathed him.

"Hey, Ma, I need something cold to drink."

Andrea kissed his eyelids. "Be right back." She closed her robe and disappeared into the kitchen. Sonia would never be that obedient.

After she toweled him off and washed up, they both went upstairs to her room. He walked into her closet and pulled out his trunk. He opened the combination lock and inspected the contents.

He grabbed the Glock 9mm and ejected the clip. He snapped the clip back in place and pulled the barrel back, putting one bullet in the chamber before he put the gun in his waistband.

"What's going on?" Andrea asked, concerned.

Brian ignored her as he pulled out the knot of cash he had in his pocket. He handed it to her. "Count it."

The only thing Andrea loved more than fucking was counting and spending money.

"It's five thousand," she said as she handed it back to him.

He put a rubber band around it and put it in the trunk. He turned on his cell phone and called Jason. "Jay, what up?"

"I'm gonna kill this bitch."

"Whoa, calm down, playa."

"Teshawna is fucking playing herself. She ain't answering her cell."

Brian shook his head. "What I told you about hitting that raw dog?"

"I was caught up in the moment and ain't have no condoms. So I said fuck it."

"Yeah, and you fucked it, and now you got your wife's cousin pregnant."

"That bitch is talking some crazy shit, Bee. She changed her mind about getting the abortion. She's saying that she'll just move back down to South Carolina, have her baby there, and I won't have to worry about a thing."

"Yeah, right," Brian said sarcastically. "Until she sees how expensive and hard it is for a sixteen-year-old to take care of a baby. She'll be calling you on the regular asking for all kinds of shit. And if you don't get it to her fast enough, she'll threaten to tell everybody who the father is. You fucked, kid."

Brian could hear Jason fuming. So he decided to change the subject. "Enough of that, did you take care of everything last night?"

"Yeah, Bee. That's all taken care of. What about Bret? Everything straight with him?"

"Yeah, no doubt. As a matter of fact, he's got something else lined up for us."

"Damn, that quick?"

"Yeah, a little venture he wants us to oversee."

"I'm wit that."

Brian's other line beeped in. He looked at the number and shook his head. "I got to go. I'm gonna call you back when I get the details." He clicked over without waiting for a response. "What's up, babe?"

Andrea rolled her eyes and left the room.

"I hate it when you do this shit," Sonia screamed. "Every time you turn your phone off, fucking Denise calls here looking for you with an attitude, and I got to put her ass in check."

"What she want now?"

"What you think she wants?" Sonia said sarcastically. "She needs formula and diapers for Christopher."

Brian sat on Andrea's bed and shook his head. "I just gave her a hundred dollars last week."

"Well, evidently, she's buying more than diapers and formula."

"If she calls back, tell her I'll be over there."

"I ain't telling her shit. What you need to do is tell her to lose my number." She hung up on him.

Brian found Andrea in the living room with her arms folded across her chest.

"We ain't gonna start this shit," Brian said.

Andrea didn't say a word.

Brian headed toward the front door.

Andrea cut in front of him. "I'm sorry, Bee. I can't help it if I get jealous.

"You ain't got nothing to be jealous about. Remember what you told me at the club the night we first met? You said you knew I would never leave my girl, and you would never ask me to. All you wanted to do was have a good time."

Andrea put her head down. "I know, but that still doesn't mean I won't get jealous."

"Look, baby," he said, as he kissed her on the cheek, "you know you're my go-to girl. If I ever need anything done, I always come to you don't I?"

She nodded.

"And do you think I would let you hold on to a trunk full of money if I didn't have faith in you?"

"No."

"So you ain't got nothing to be jealous about because you have a position in my heart that Sonia could never have."

Traces of a grin appeared on her lips.

"I got to go, okay?"

Brian kissed her on her cheek and gave her a long hug before heading out the door.

Chapter 8

On the ride to Denise's house, Brian got into the ritual of mentally preparing himself to deal with the family.

Denise, the youngest of three sisters, had a family largely composed of women. All of her sisters had multiple children by multiple baby daddies. Brian refused to be like them dudes—subservient to their every command.

He felt he didn't owe her anything. He couldn't understand how she could get pregnant off a one-night stand. What are the odds?

When he broke fool and said he wasn't going to be a father, she asked him for five hundred dollars so she could go get an abortion.

Seven months later, at a party he was at with Sonia, she walked in eight months pregnant. He was fuming. So much so that when she got up to go to the ladies' room, he followed her inside and made her feel dirtier than dirt.

The only reason he gave her money was because Sonia made him. And the only reason why he told

Sonia was because he knew one day Denise would use her pregnancy as a means to break them up.

As he pulled up to the house, all of Denise's sister's kids were outside playing.

Veronica, Denise's cousin, was the first one to see him.

"Dee-Dee, your baby daddy is here."

Veronica shot the first line of questioning at him. "Why Dee-Dee got to be calling all over town looking for you?"

Brian knew he had no wins when it came to having the last word, so he did the opposite. He ignored her.

"Forget you then," Veronica said with an attitude.

Denise sat on the couch, rocking Christopher to sleep. She immediately stood up and handed him to Brian.

"I'm tired of going through this with you, Brian"

"Going through what?"

"You not coming around unless I call, you not giving me any money unless I ask."

He wanted to say so many hurtful things to her, shit that had been welling up inside of him for months, but he knew it would do nothing but bring down the family's wrath on him.

"How much you need?"

"A hundred and fifty dollars."

"A hundred and fifty dollars?" he shouted, waking Christopher up. "A hundred and fifty dollars for what?"

"Food, diapers, and clothes. In case you haven't noticed, he's growing every day."

He handed his son back to her and dug into his pocket. "Here's fifty," he said, peeling off two twenties and a ten.

"Oh, no, he didn't," Gwen, Denise's older sister, said.

Brian turned toward her. "Gwen, you need to mind your business."

"You ain't gonna talk to me like I'm one of them chicken heads you be messing with."

They both stared each other down.

Brian was first to speak. "Fuck this. I'm out of here."

"Get to stepping, cheap ass nigga," Gwen said, shoving him.

Brian turned his attention to Denise. "Stop calling Sonia. She ain't got nothing to do with you and I."

Denise looked to the ground.

"Don't let that nigga talk to you like that, Dee-Dee."

Brian's lips curled in disgust toward Gwen. "You need to grow up and stop cursing in front of these kids and check your baby daddies. Last I checked, they both be smacking the dog shit out of you."

Gwen charged at Brian with balled fists.

Fed up with all the bullshit, he shoved her on her ass.

Denise screamed at him, "Get the fuck out of here, Brian." Brian stood his ground.

"I'm serious, get out of my house." Denise's yelling made Christopher cry.

Brian stormed out of the house and left.

Chapter 9

Manny pulled up to the brownstone. Broken glass from the Lincoln Navigator truck was still in the street.

The police were still canvassing the neighborhood looking for any leads or evidence to the double homicide that took place a few nights ago.

Manny hit the top button on the intercom when he got to the top of the steps.

An irritated voice came from the intercom. "Who dat?"

"Manny."

The irritated voice buzzed him in.

Tequan sat in the living room still in his robe, drinking from a bottle of Hennessy when Manny walked in.

"What's the word?" Tequan asked.

"According to old man Armstead down the block, he saw three dudes pulling off in a black SUV. The truck was probably stolen, so it makes no sense trying to track it down."

Tequan threw the bottle of Hennessy against the wall. "I don't care what you got to do. You find them motherfuckers."

He stood and paced back and forth. "One of my people got murdered right on my doorstep. You know what that's like? That's like a nigga telling me to suck his dick. Who in all the five boroughs got the balls to tell me to suck their dick?"

Manny listened to him as he vented about the unimaginable pain he was going to inflict on the motherfuckers who robbed and murdered his lieutenant.

Tequan felt that the streets were sending him a message, and he was damn sure going to answer back. "What's up with Jennifer and Paula?" he asked.

Manny opened his cell phone and dialed their number.

Jennifer and Paula were the best females in Manny's stable. They were the masters of their trade. They could hook a crook or baller and fuck any information out of them.

Jennifer picked up on the second ring. "Hello?"

"Y'all hear anything yet?"

"Nobody knows shit, just rumors on what happened. Whoever did it had enough sense not to brag about it."

Tequan got frustrated listening to the one-sided conversation. "Did they hear anything?"

Manny ignored him. "Yeah, I'll see you later tonight." He hung up.

"So what's going on?" Tequan asked.

"Everybody seems to be in the dark like us."

Tequan now focused his anger on Manny. "Everyone's in the dark like us? I pay you a quarter of a million a year to be in the dark like everyone else? Is that what you're telling me?"

"I will find them before the week is out," Manny said. "Believe that."

Manny had already formulated a course of action. Henry had two pickups that night, one in Queens and the other in the Bronx. Manny knew that sometimes the only way to find the source was to work your way backward. He would start with Henry's last pickup.

Chapter 10

Brian got home just before sundown and was surprised to see his mother sitting at the dining room table. "Ma, what up?"

"What happened to you today?"

The heat of shame rushed to his face. "I'm sorry, Ma. I forgot."

"How could you forget, Brian? I reminded you all week. I reminded you this morning before you ran out of here."

"I know, but it just slipped my mind."

His mother opened the folder that was lying in front of her. "Thank God I was able to talk Jean into giving me the job application for you to fill out. You're going to do it right now."

"But I'm on my way back out. Sonia and I are going to a play tonight."

"You're not going anywhere 'til you fill out this application."

Brian moaned, "C'mon, Ma. Why can't you do it? You know all my information."

"I'm going out my way to get you this job at the hospital. The least you could do is give me the respect and take fifteen minutes out of your precious time to fill out this application."

Brian knew he had no wins. He sat down and began filling it out. "What does DOB mean?"

"Your date of birth."

A few seconds went by.

"Ma, what's my Social Security number?"

His mother shook her head. "How did you graduate from high school?"

"Graduating ain't got nothing to do with my Social Security number."

"It's got everything to do with it. You can't even fill out a job application. How do you expect to make it in the real world if you can't even fill out a job application?"

"I'm in the real world now, and I'm doing pretty well."

"Is that so?"

"Yeah, that's so."

"Well, let's see. You're eighteen years old and never worked a real job. You have a four-month-old son by a girl you didn't even know before you slept with her, you're living at home with your parents, and the only thing that seems to be important to you is clothes, jewelry, and your Nissan Pathfinder. All of which your father and I have no idea where you get the money to buy all of that stuff. Correction, we do have an idea, but you always deny it."

"Are we going to go through this again? I'm not selling drugs. And if I were, Dad would know, being that he's a cop and all. And I told you that I work construction off the books. They don't want to hire me because of my felony conviction."

"Oh, yes. The gun that you got caught with that you swore wasn't yours."

"It wasn't mine. I asked my friend if I could look at it and when he handed it to me, the police rolled up on us and caught me with it."

"I must really look like I got *dummy* written on my forehead," she said.

"Y'all can believe what you want, but I know what I'm doing and what I'm not doing."

They sat in silence as he finished filling out the application.

Chapter 11

Brian finally pulled up to Sonia's house later that night. Ordinarily, he would honk the horn for her to come out, but he knew her parents were home, and he wouldn't hear the end of it if he didn't come in and say hi.

He ran up the front steps and rang the bell. He could hear the TV in the living room. Most likely her father was sitting in his favorite chair with a Budweiser in his hand watching ESPN.

Sonia's mother answered the door.

"What's good, Ma?" Brian asked, giving her a hug.

"I'm fine. How are you?"

"Couldn't be better."

She inspected his clothes. "You looking sharp there."

"I got to. I don't want your daughter breaking up with me because I dress like a bum."

"Boy, you stupid. Get in here."

Brian walked into the living room. "How you doing, Mr. Ingram?"

Sonia's father stared at him for a moment and then took a swallow of his Budweiser before answering. "Mmm, hmm."

Sonia's father always made Brian feel uneasy around him, but that was the plan.

Sonia told Brian on plenty of occasions that her father liked him. He just had a funny way of showing it.

Brian never got that impression. He always walked on eggshells around him.

Sonia appeared at the top of the stairs.

Brian couldn't help but marvel at how she made any outfit look good.

When he first met her, she was a quiet Coke-bottle-glasses-wearing bookworm. One day, he rolled up to Springfield High, and there she was in front of the school, scrapping.

She was on top of a girl twice her size, beating her relentlessly. When the crowd tried pulling her off the chick, she started swinging at them.

She struggled to get to her book bag, but her friend wouldn't give it to her. He heard somebody say, "She's trying to get to her box cutter." That day, he knew he had to have her. She was official.

Sonia ran down the stairs and into Brian's tensed arms and kissed him on the lips.

He cut his eyes at her father and smiled nervously.

Sonia turned to her parents. "I promise I'll call if I'm not back by midnight."

When Brian got into the SUV and started it, he exhaled.

"What's your problem?" Sonia asked.

"Your pops be on some shit."

"He's keeping you in check. That's what fathers are supposed to do."

"Yeah, whatever."

Sonia massaged the inside of his thigh. "We're going to enjoy ourselves tonight, right?"

Brian didn't respond verbally, but she felt him rising in his pants. She leaned over and licked the inside of his ear.

Brian was putty in her hands.

"Yes, baby, we're going to enjoy ourselves," he finally responded.

Chapter 12

Brian jumped out of his sleep when the hotel phone rang. "Hello?"

"This is your five o'clock wake-up call, sir."

Brian rubbed his eyes. "Okay, thanks."

He rolled back over and wrapped himself around Sonia's naked body.

"Brian, when are you going to start living for us and stop living for yourself?"

Where did that come from? Brian thought.

"What are you talking about, baby?"

Sonia turned to face him. "I'm talking about you getting a job or possibly going back to school."

"Baby, go back to sleep. We still got a couple of hours."

Sonia sat up. "I'm serious, Brian."

"Let's talk about this later," he said, pointing to the window. "Look, it's still dark out."

"We have to talk about this now. I have to know if you're willing to settle down and do right by me,"

Sonia said, putting her head on his chest. "Because I'm pregnant."

The weekend finally came and not a moment too soon. Brian was stressed to the max. After Sonia dropped the bomb about her pregnancy, he had to sit with her when she dropped it on her parents.

After Sonia and her mother pried her father's hands from around Brian's neck, they all sat in silence. Brian decided to leave and give Sonia and her parent's time to come to grips with the situation.

He called Devon and Jason and told them to meet him on the block.

Chapter 13

While waiting for Devon and Jason to show up, Brian kicked it with some of the young bucks who were no more than twelve to thirteen years old. They were big for their ages, but their innocent eyes always gave them away.

"The eyes are the windows to the soul." At least that's what Brian heard. One thing he knew for sure was when you start running the streets, the eyes are the last thing to harden.

Right now, their eyes are wide with excitement. Soon, their eyes will be beady with resentment.

They had dreams of becoming the next Fat Cat or Tommy Montana.

These kids didn't even finish junior high. They couldn't complete a sentence without saying, "You heard?" And when they couldn't think of the word to describe what they were talking about, they just called it "the shit" or "the jump off."

Jason and Devon pulled up in Jason's Toyota Camry.

Brian hopped in the back, and they drove to their favorite hang out.

PS 30 school yard was a source of comfort for them. From the first grade to the fifth, they were kids, oblivious to the streets and all its entrapments. All they wanted to do was play and watch cartoons.

Back in the fourth grade, he saw a group of kids beating the piss out of Devon and Jason. He was laughing his ass off until he saw one of the kids pick up a bottle. There's nothing wrong with beating someone down, but they were taking it too far.

Brian ran up on the kid and snuffed him. The gang swarmed him like a pack of wolves, then attacked. He held his own as best he could.

For every punch he got off, five came back at him. Finally, the teachers rushed in and pulled them apart. The next day when he saw the dudes that jumped him, they nodded. He had their respect. And from that day, he couldn't get rid of Jason or Devon.

Devon took a few swallows of his Heineken before speaking his mind. "So what's the big venture Jay can't stop talking about?"

"I'm meeting up with Bret later this week to finalize everything; but from what I've seen so far, he's hooked up with some Long Island cats who have agreed to cut him a piece of their pie."

"Why would they do that? What's the catch?" Jay asked.

Until that moment, Brian hadn't given it any thought. "Like I said, I got to see him later on this week to finalize everything."

Brian could see the weary look on their faces. "The spot is pumping ten thousand every weekend, guaranteed."

Both their faces lit up.

"Now for the fucked-up news," Brian said.

Devon and Jason cocked their heads.

"Sonia is pregnant."

"Oh shit, Bee," Jason busted out.

"Cool," Devon said.

"No, that's not cool, y'all. And she's gonna have it."

"Yo, Bee," Jason said, "ain't nothing wrong with that."

"Nigga, I know you ain't talking. You two steps away from giving Teshawna that abortion yourself."

"That's totally different, Bee. That's my wife's cousin. If wifey was pregnant, I would be happier than a motherfucker."

Brian took a swallow of his beer. "Yeah, well, I'm not happy, motherfucker. I got Denise breathing down my neck for diapers, formula, and all kinds of shit; my mom is sweating me about working at the hospital with her; my pops is talking some enlisting in the army shit; and now Sonia wants me to settle down, maybe even get married." He finished off his first bottle of beer and opened another. "It seems like no one cares what I want to do with my life."

"What do you want to do?" Devon asked.

"I don't know, but that doesn't give people the right to live my life for me. I'm not even twenty years old yet, and I feel like I'm going through a midlife crisis."

Jason pulled out his cell and hit speed dial.

"Who you calling?" Brian asked.

Jason hung up. "Fucking bitch is still avoiding my calls."

"You still tripping over Teshawna?" Brian asked.

Jason hit another number on his speed dial. "Hey, sweetheart, what's up?" He was talking to Laquana, wifey.

"Where you at, boy?"

"I'm a couple blocks away."

"I haven't heard from you all day. Where you been?"

"I've been with Brian all day. He got some good news, so we celebrating. Sonia's pregnant."

Brian swatted Jason's head.

"You serious, baby? My girl is pregnant? Oh my god!"

Jason pulled the phone from his ear. "Okay, sweetheart, calm down. When's the next time you and Teshawna going to the mall to get your nails done?"

"Tomorrow afternoon. Why?"

"Remember them red and gold New Balances I wanted?"

"Yeah."

"Pick them up for me."

"Yeah, all right. That's it? You don't want a shirt to go with them?"

"Nah, just the sneakers, baby."

"Okay, whatever."

"I gotta go. Brian and the fellas are waiting for me. I'll swing around the crib in a few."

Jason hung up with a smirk on his face.

"What, nigga?" Brian asked him.

"Teshawna is going to be at the mall tomorrow afternoon with Laquana."

"And?" Devon said.

Jason didn't answer.

Brian shook his head. "What you planning to do, Jay?"

All Jason did was smile.

Chapter 14

Supreme pulled up to the Dynasty, the hottest club in all the five boroughs.

He stepped out his platinum-colored Infiniti SUV, knowing all eyes were on him.

He sat at his regular both in the VIP section, ordered a Bacardi and Coke, and watched the honeys shake and bounce their asses on the dance floor.

Supreme was Chuka's right-hand man. Chuka had half The Bronx sewed up. He had drug spots in damn near every project, and he had the leaders of all The Bronx gangs on his payroll.

Supreme nodded and winked at the bodacious babes vying for his attention. *Hoes are so shallow,* he thought to himself. They wore Lycra, microminis, and sheer shirts that left nothing for the imagination.

For the past hour and a half, he kept eyeing a sister who was also sitting in the VIP section in the booth right across from him. She was by herself, but she constantly glanced at her watch, which told him she was waiting for someone. Her elegant tailored dress accentuating her curves and hinting at her long legs had his imagination racing. Her facial features were intoxicating. Her forehead, nose, cheeks, and lips commanded attention like an Egyptian goddess. Yet her eyes and bashful smile she flashed when their eyes met conveyed the shyness of a virgin on her wedding night.

He finally decided to wave at her.

She looked beyond him like he didn't exist.

Supreme could feel his face turning red with embarrassment. *Who the fuck she think she is, he thought to himself. She must not know who the fuck I am. I should walk right up to her and punch her in the face. I bet then she'll know.* Supreme's attraction for her intensified by 200 percent. She wasn't the average shallow hoe looking for a baller to fuck and suck for his dough. She was different. He had to have her.

He picked up his drink and walked over to her booth. "I hate when this happens."

She looked up at him. "Excuse me?"

He pointed to his drink. "You pay an arm and a leg for a drink and two minutes later it's hot."

She smiled at him. "Yeah, I know what you mean."

He motioned for the waitress. "Let me buy you a fresh drink."

She eyed her drink as if really considering his offer. "No, I'm okay."

"Please, I insist."

The waitress walked up. "Can I get you something?"

"Yes," Supreme said. "I'll have another Bacardi and Coke on the rocks. And miss here will have a—"

She looked at him then to her drink. "I'll have Sex on the Beach." Supreme blinked. *Did she just hit me with a subliminal message?* he thought to himself.

He sat down and took a gulp of his Bacardi with Coke.

"I don't think that's a good idea, I'm waiting for someone."

"I'm just keeping you company 'til he arrives. No harm in that, right?"

She glanced at her watch. "I guess not."

The waitress brought their drinks.

Supreme took a long swallow before he spoke, "So what's your name?" He was mesmerized by the way she mouthed her name.

"Jennifer."

Chapter 15

When Brian pulled up to Bret's house, he saw Bret's mother planting flowers in the front yard.

Trish's eyes lit up when she saw him. "Hi, Brian."

Her mother looked up and smiled when she saw him. "Hey, baby. How you doing?"

"Hey, Mrs. Davis. I'm fine. How are you?"

"Tired and hot," she said, wiping the sweat from her forehead. "I've been out here all morning planting these flowers all around the house, and Trisha ain't helping me none."

Trish rolled her eyes. "I brought those heavy ass bags of dirt over here."

"Girl," her mother said, throwing a handful of dirt at her, "what I told you about cursing in front of me?"

Brian cut in. "Trish, your brother inside?"

He could see the look of disappointment on her face.

"He's in his room."

"Mrs. Davis, you mind if I go in and—"

"Sure, baby. Go on ahead."

"I'm going inside to get something to drink," Trish said.

She cut in front of Brian so she could sway her hips in front of him. As soon as they walked in, she turned around and kissed him on the lips.

"Why you ain't been coming around to see me?" she asked.

"I've been busy."

"I bet you find time for Sonia."

"You sound like you jealous."

"Fuck you."

"I tell you what. I'm going to a beach party in Far Rockaway next weekend. How 'bout I swing by and get you, and we'll go together?"

She folded her hands and rolled her eyes. "Yeah, whatever." Brian shook his head and went upstairs.

Bret was sitting on the edge of his bed, puffing on a blunt, and talking to himself. There were rumors circulating that Bret was lacing his weed with crack. Brian didn't believe them until now, because the shit he was smelling at the moment didn't smell like regular weed. It smelled like burning plastic and rubbing alcohol.

"Bret, what up?"

Bret's head jerked up. "You scared the shit out of me," he snapped. "You should've called and told me you were coming."

"I wasn't really planning on stopping by. I was just in the neighborhood, so I said fuck it. Let me touch base with you."

Bret smashed the blunt out in his ashtray and shuffled to his closet. He dug in one of his coat pockets and pulled out a card.

He shuffled back to the bed and sat down. "Here," he said, holding the card out to Brian.

Brian grabbed it and memorized the address.

"What's this?"

"Go here tonight and pick up the shit. They'll be expecting you." Bret picked up the blunt and lit it back up.

"Hey, Bret. Let me ask you a question."

Bret stared at Brian through hazy eyes.

"What are you doing for them Long Island cats in order for them to be cutting you a large piece of their pie?"

Brian's question took a moment to sink in.

"It's not what I'm doing," Bret said laughing. "It's what you're going to be doing."

"And what am I supposed to be doing?"

Bret took a long pull off his blunt. "You're gonna do what you do best. I need you to rob a spot."

"What the hell are you talking about?"

"Hold on, Bee. This ain't just no crack-dealing spot. This is the spot. I'm talking a minimum of fifty kilos of coke and at least five hundred thousand in cash, guaranteed."

"You're out of your mind, Bret. You smoking too much of that shit."

Bret blinked and got to his feet. "What the fuck are you talking about? This ain't nothing new. I set the spots up and you rob them."

"Little holes in the wall, Bret. A spot holding fifty kilos and half a million dollars ain't no hole in the wall."

"Listen, Bee. These LI cats already did their homework. They even got somebody on the inside.

Brian's face filled with doubt. "I don't know, Bret. You may trust them dudes, but I don't."

"That's why you're going there tonight. Not just to protect my vested interest but to also familiarize yourself with the dynamics."

Brian shook his head.

"Name your price, Bee."

"It's not about the money."

"Bullshit. Tell me how much you want for this job, and I'll make sure you'll get it."

Bret knew how to reel Brian in.

Brian thought for a moment. "I want the money. All of it."

"Get the fuck out of here."

"Half a million is a drop in the ocean compared to the millions you'll make off of the keys of coke."

Bret took another long pull on his blunt.

With all the shit happening in his life, Brian figured he'd go for broke. With a half a mill, he could start a legit business and become a millionaire at the age of twenty-five. For the first time in his life, he wasn't nearsighted. He could see past twenty-one, and it was looking pretty good.

Bret must have seen the future as well because he was nodding his head. "All right, you got a deal. You keep the money, and I get the coke."

"That's what I'm talking about," Brian said smiling.

Brian gave him a pound and headed downstairs.

Trish was in the living room watching soap operas. "So you off to do some work for my brother?"

Brian knew how to weave her cheap shots. "Stay out of grown folk's business, little girl."

"Was I a little girl when you came in my mouth three weeks ago?"

He couldn't weave that one. "Keep your voice down. What the fuck is wrong with you?"

"In case you haven't noticed, little girls have big mouths."

Red flashed before his eyes. "I'm out of here, you bugging out."

"Go on, then."

Brian said his goodbyes to Mrs. Davis and headed to the address on the card to pick up Bret's package.

Chapter 16

Supreme had Jennifer wrapped around his finger in no time. He made her laugh, and he made her feel comfortable enough to open up to him and tell him all of her problems and misfortune with men. She even got a little teary-eyed at times.

"Where have you been?" Jennifer said to the person standing behind him.

He turned around, and his jaw almost hit the ground. Behind him stood an exact replica of Jennifer.

"I'm sorry, babe. My relief called in sick so I was stuck in that nursing home 'til someone finally came to relieve me."

"You could have called instead of having me sit here all by myself waiting for you."

"It doesn't look like you're sitting by yourself."

Supreme was in shock. He kept looking at Jennifer and then back to her twin.

She wore a white two-piece suit that hugged her curves and caressed her breasts.

Jennifer tapped Supreme on the shoulder. "As you've probably guessed, this is my sister, Paula."

Supreme shook her hand.

"And, Paula, this is Supreme."

Supreme stood up. "Please sit down. I was...I was just...."

He turned to Jennifer. "I thought you were waiting for your man."

"I never said that. You said that."

Supreme was speechless.

Paula interrupted. "I'm thirsty."

Supreme waved the waitress over.

"Can I get you something, sir?"

"Yes, my lady friend here would like—"

"Sex on the Beach, please."

Supreme's heart fluttered. For a moment, he envisioned the three of them wrapped in a blanket on Jones Beach. He was never the type to spend money on hoes, but tonight, he would spend all his money, sell his clothes and his truck for a chance to be with the both of them.

A few drinks later, he was sitting between the tipsy twins, bragging about his and Chuka's enterprise.

Jennifer's hand slid down to the inside of his thigh. He lost his train of thought. Without warning, she kissed him on the lips.

"I know you didn't just kiss that man," Paula said. "You don't even know him."

Jennifer giggled. "I don't have to know him to kiss him."

Supreme defended her. "Yeah, she don't have to know me to give me a little sugar."

"You crazy, girl," Paula said. Then with a devilish grin, she asked, "Is he any good?"

"He's real good," Jennifer purred.

"Did he get your panties wet?"

"Soaked."

"Whoa! Whoa! Whoa! Hold on," Supreme cut in. "How y'all just gonna talk about me like I'm not even here?"

They both looked at him and laughed.

"I'm sorry," Jennifer said. "Forgive me."

Jennifer kept massaging his thigh.

"Well?" Paula said to Supreme.

"Well, what?"

"Can I get my panties wet too?"

Supreme's throat was too dry for his words to come up. He looked over at Jennifer.

She gave him the go-for-it nod.

He turned back to Paula and kissed her gently on the lips.

She moaned with pleasure and grabbed his hand and put it on her stiffening nipple.

Supreme couldn't believe what was happening. Shit like this didn't even happen in his wildest dreams. He'd already written their destiny. He was going to be the first nigga in the hood to have kids with twins.

They'll be living in the same house and sharing the same bed.

Jennifer dried up his wet dream.

"Paula, we got to go."

"What?" Supreme said alarmed.

"What are you talking about, girl?" Paula said.

"I think we had a little too much to drink, and we might do something we'll both regret."

"Girl, please. When you live your life to the fullest, you never have any regrets."

"You don't even know him."

"That ain't stop you from sticking your tongue in his mouth and feeling his dick."

Supreme couldn't believe how they could talk about him as if he wasn't even there.

"If you can kiss him and feel on his dick, I can fuck him." Jennifer put her head down in embarrassment.

Paula continued. "I don't know about you, but I need to let off some steam tonight. Like right now."

He could smell the lust emanating from her pores.

Jennifer looked up at him.

Supreme shrugged his shoulders. "Hey, I'm down for whatever."

Jennifer turned her glass up, finishing off her drink. "Fuck it. Let's go."

Chapter 17

Brian examined the scenery on his way to Long Island. It didn't look the same. It was dark out. The landscape seemed to have taken on a whole different theme, a theme that he was used to. He saw chicks wearing Daisy Duke shorts and long weaves. He saw a few dudes on every other corner, crouched down shooting dice, and drinking beers wrapped in brown paper bags.

As he pulled up to the strip bar, he saw Powerful and a mob of dudes posted up on the corner. He turned down a side street and parked. He hopped out and walked back down to the corner with the meanest bop he could muster. He made a beeline to Powerful. Dudes parted the way, making him feel like he was walking through a gauntlet. Between the stares, snarls, and mumbling, he felt like he was walking on marked territory.

Powerful walked toward him, flashing a mouth full of gold teeth. "Peace, god. What up?" he embraced Brian like he was his long lost brother.

Brian hugged him back and smiled.

Once the crew saw the embrace, their stares soft-ened, but their guards were still up.

"So what the deal?" Powerful asked. "How much you got?"

"Ten G-packs."

Powerful nodded. "Okay." He called over one of his little men and whispered something in his ear.

The little man ran off down the block.

"So how does this work?" Brian asked.

"We gonna keep it real simple, Bee. My people are going to knock off the packs. If Robo see any dudes who don't belong from around here, he's go-ing to fuck with us. That's why Bret's little boys got harassed that night. When they knock off your ten Ps, you'll get your ten Gs."

Brian was lost. "So you're not selling from a house? You're going to knock off the G-packs on a street corner?"

"Chill, Bee," Powerful said, putting his arm around him. "We got store fronts, houses, and corners, but you don't need to know where and how many. All you need to know is you'll have ten Gs in your hand in four hours."

Brian looked skeptical. "So what do we do 'til then?"

Powerful looked toward the strip bar. "We're gonna hang out.

Chapter 18

Supreme couldn't get to the hotel quick enough with his future baby mamas.

They stripped down to their bras and panties, then slowly undressed him as they whispered in his ear what they ware going to do to him. They stretched him out on the bed, then removed their bras and panties. Jennifer was the first to hop on top of him and kiss him on the lips.

He felt Paula tugging his underwear off. Jennifer kept the rhythm going. She rubbed her dripping wet pussy along the length of his penis. He was in heaven.

Then he heard a click. His eyes popped open, surprised to see that Jennifer had handcuffed both his hands to the bedpost.

Just as he was about to panic, Paula took his whole manhood in her mouth. He closed his eyes, he was in heaven again.

Then he heard another click.

He didn't open his eyes until he felt the cold steel jammed against his cheek.

Jennifer and Paula hopped off him.

Supreme cut his eyes at the man holding the gun to his face. "Hey, Manny. What the fuck man? What's going on?"

"I was kinda hoping you could tell me."

Chapter 19

Brian and Powerful walked into the strip bar and headed toward the back.

Equality and Knowledge were getting lap dances by two young, succulent, and curvaceous girls. He now understood the workings of the club. In the afternoons, the old and dried-up chicks worked the joint. But at night, prime time, the fresh flesh came on the scene. None of them looked to be a minute over eighteen.

Three drinks and five lap dances later, Powerful tapped Equality on the shoulder and whispered something in his ear.

Equality nodded and dug into his pocket and handed him a set of keys.

"C'mon, yo," Powerful said. "Let's go get some trees."

Brian and Powerful hopped in Equality's truck and drove to the dry cleaners. Powerful cut the engine off and jumped out.

Weed sold inside a dry cleaners? Brian thought. *LI was the twilight zone for real.*

Five minutes later, Powerful walked out and hopped into the truck. He handed Brian the brown paper bag and started the engine. "Smell that shit, Bee," he said.

Weed wasn't Brian's thing. He smoked it a couple times, but he never felt the buzz everyone bragged about.

He opened the bag and sniffed it. "Yo, this shit stink."

"That's skunk, Bee."

He wasn't lying. That's exactly what it smelled like. Brian noticed that Powerful was headed in the opposite direction of the strip club.

"Where we headed?"

"We about to roll that skunk and get it crunk."

Brian stretched and brushed his hand across his Glock tucked in his waistband. He touched it to reassure himself that if anything went down, he was going out blazing.

They finally pulled up to a house. The lights were dim. It was dead silent outside, so Brian could hear the faint thump of music coming from inside.

Powerful shut the engine off. "C'mon, Bee, everybody's inside."

Brian got out the truck and looked around. "Whose house is this?"

"It's ours. Well, actually, it's Mr. Smith's. He's a crack head. E-qual be giving him a couple bottles to let us use his spot, you know?"

"Yeah, no doubt."

Powerful grabbed the bag from Brian and walked toward the house.

So this is what these cats do? They get together and smoke trees? Brian thought to himself. *Well, who knows,* he thought, *maybe they brought some chicks with them. After all, what would a party be without chicks?*

When Powerful opened the door, the music, laughter, and funk hit Brian in the face. From the outside, it looked like there were only a handful of people up in the house. As they walked in, it looked like everyone from the strip club and the corner was up in there, and the chicks weren't the only ones stripping. The majority of the dudes only had on their boxers and socks, and the chicks were dancing in their panties and out of them.

Fuck what I said about LI, Brian thought. *This is where it's at.*

"Gimme the Light" by Sean Paul was pumping on the sound system. Powerful waved at E-qual and pointed to the brown paper bag. E-qual threw his fist in the air. "Roll that shit up, nigga," he shouted over the music.

Powerful flagged down two of his little men, who were no more than ten or eleven years old, and handed them the bag and told them to go in the backroom and roll it all up.

"Y'all got anything to drink up in here?" Brian shouted to Powerful.

"Check the fridge, Bee. There's got to be something in there." He pointed him in the direction of the kitchen.

On his way to the kitchen, Brian grabbed some tits and rubbed on some asses, expecting the females to swat his hands away. Not only did their devilish grins broaden, but some of them boldly grabbed his crotch and giggled.

Fuck what I said about LI, Brian thought. *This is where it's at.*

By the time he made it to the fridge, he was bulging in his pants. There wasn't shit in the fridge but a box of Arm and Hammer baking soda.

Everybody had a drink but him. Out of the corner of his eye, he spotted a chick turning up a forty ounce and guzzling it like she was a dude. When she turned the bottle down, it was half gone. Brian was in love. He danced his way over to her, keeping eye contact all the while. When he danced up in front of her, she smiled and put her head down.

Brian touched her chin and lifted her head up. "Oh, no. Don't be shy now. I saw the way you turned that forty up. Let me get some of that." He grabbed the bottle from her and took a couple swallows then handed it back to her.

She grabbed the bottle and turned it up.

"Why you so quiet, Ma?"

"No reason."

In a matter of seconds, the whole house smelled like a skunk just let loose.

Shorty with the forty whipped her head around trying to track down the source. "They got weed up in here?"

"Calm down, Ma. I got you." Brian grabbed her by the hand and made a beeline to the backroom.

He snatched a blunt off the table, lit it up, and passed it to her.

As they headed to the living room, she took a pull. She pulled and pulled and pulled.

Brian's eyes almost popped out of their sockets. "Damn, Ma, what the fuck?"

She held her breath and passed him the blunt.

He tried to take a pull, but the shit burned his lips. She steamed the motherfucker.

As she exhaled a cloud of smoke, she started unbuttoning her shirt. She stripped to the music and giggled a couple of times when she saw Brian drooling.

He held what was left of the blunt to her lips and let her steam it, 'til the fire burned his fingertips.

He dropped it and sucked his fingers. She pulled his fingers out of his mouth and sucked on them.

He grabbed her by the butt and pulled her to him. He kissed her hard on the lips, and he could taste "fuck me" on her tongue. He felt someone staring at the back of his neck so he turned around. He saw Equality grinning at him.

Equality threw his fist in the air.

Brian did the same thing before pulling hot girl into the backroom. He busted in on the two kids rolling the blunts. "Y'all got to find some place else to roll that shit, you heard?"

The kids stared at him like he was speaking in tongues.

He grabbed the bag off the table and started stuffing the weed into it. "Take your asses into the bathroom and roll this shit." He shoved them out of the room, and then focused his attention back to the petite chick who was now crawling on all fours on the bed.

Petite isn't part of my criteria, Brian thought. But she met the other two, female and fuckable.

He turned his back to her, so she couldn't see him pull the gun out of his waistband and put it in the dresser drawer. The bedroom was a lot brighter than the rest of the house. He finally got a good look at his freak for the night. Through the haze of the weed and alcohol, Brian still picked up on her innocence. Her petite body and giggling hit him in the stomach so hard that he almost doubled over. How old was this chick?

He thought back to the way she guzzled that forty ounce of Old Gold and steamed that weed. No young chick could do that.

The lust and experience he saw in her eyes when she sucked his fingers couldn't have been in the eyes of a fourteen-year-old.

She looked at him with a confused expression. The bulge in his pants told her that he was ready to jump on her, but his facial expression said something different.

He kept thinking back to the beer, weed, and the finger sucking. *Fuck it,* he thought. *Even if she was fourteen, he wouldn't be the first one she's been with. Besides, she wants it.*

When he walked toward the bed, she started smiling. Yeah, she wanted it, but Brian didn't know what possessed him to open his mouth. "How old are you, Ma?"

His question made her blink. "I'm old enough," she said rubbing the bulge in his pants.

Alarms, bells, sirens, horns, and lights went off in Brian's head.

He backed away from her and left the room. He weaved through the crowd of half-naked chicks and dudes, trying to find Powerful. As he took a good look at some of the females, he realized most of them were way too young.

He finally spotted Powerful in a corner pressed up on a female, whispering in her ear. He kept calling his name as he walked toward him. "Yo, P. I got to get back to my truck."

One of his eyebrows shot up. "Why? What's up?"

"I left my cell phone, and I know wifey is calling off the hook."

"You want to use the phone?"

"Nah, I just want to get my cell, because I'm also expecting a call from Bret."

Powerful didn't move. It became obvious that the chick he was pressed up on was about to give him some.

"Listen," Brian said. "It'll only take five minutes."

He looked at the girl. "You want to go for a ride?"

She responded. "I don't care."

"Okay, Bee. Let me tell the gods where we're going."

As they reached the front door, Brian remembered that he left his gun in the dresser drawer.

"Yo, P. Hold on, I forgot something in the back."

He made his way to the backroom. When he got there, the door was closed, but he thought nothing of it. When he opened it, he jumped. There on the bed, E-qual had the young chick with her legs spread to their breaking point.

He was pounding into her like a jackhammer. The girl didn't even notice him walk in. She winced every time Equality rammed into her.

E-qual noticed him right away and smirked. "You change your mind, god? You want some of this when I'm done?"

Brian spun around and headed to the front door. If he had gotten to his gun, he probably would've shot Equality in the ass.

On their way to Brian's truck, Powerful told him the good news. "We took care of that, Bee."

Brian looked at his watch. "It's only been three hours."

"Actually, they were done an hour ago."

"So why you only telling me now?"

"You were enjoying yourself at the party, so I said fuck it, I let you enjoy yourself."

How the fuck could these dudes knock off ten G-packs in two hours? Brian thought.

"Well, I guess I don't have to come back tomorrow night then."

"You can come back if you want. We can hang out and shit like that."

"I just might take you up on that offer," Brian said.

When they pulled up to Brian's truck, one of Powerful's little men approached with a black knapsack. He handed it to Powerful, and Powerful handed it to Brian. "It's all there, Bee."

Brian climbed into his truck and counted it. "This is incredible."

Brian had enough for one night. He had to get his bearings back. "Yo, P. I'm gonna call it a night. I'm heading back to Queens to rest my head."

"Damn, Bee. You just got out here. It's not even eleven o'clock yet."

"Nah, P. I'm out. I will swing by tomorrow night though."

"We'll be waiting on you. Peace, god."

"Peace."

Chapter 20

The anticipation of death had Supreme trembling.

Manny dramatically pulled the .38 snub-nosed revolver away from Supreme's cheek and opened the barrel. He exposed the empty gun to Supreme who then forced a nervous smile on his face.

Manny then dug into his pocket and pulled out a single bullet and put it in the barrel.

Supreme's eyes widened when Manny slapped the barrel shut and spun it.

"Yo, Manny," Supreme pleaded, "tell me what this is about? Whatever you need to know, I'll tell you."

Manny stared at him, letting the severity of the situation sink in. "Tell me about the niggas responsible for murdering Henry."

Supreme had a confused look on his face, but then he put two and two together. "Yo, Manny, I ain't have nothing to do with that. I heard about it, but I swear I had nothing to do with that."

Manny looked over at Jennifer and Paula who were now fully dressed in black denim suits with their hair pulled back in single pony tails.

Jennifer was the first to speak. "He's lying. He told me at the club that nothing goes down in the five boroughs without him knowing about it."

"I was fucking trying to impress you, bitch," Supreme shouted in between sobs.

Manny studied him for a moment, then shook his head. He put the gun to Supreme's head, shielded his face with is left hand, and pulled the trigger.

"No!" Supreme shouted.

Click!

Jennifer and Paula busted out laughing as Supreme shitted himself. He didn't give a damn about pride, honor, or manhood. All he cared about was walking out of there alive.

"Manny, please, God, please. I swear on my mother all I know is what I heard on the street," Supreme pleaded.

Manny shook his head.

Supreme cried uncontrollably when Manny dug into his pocket and pulled out another bullet. He snapped open the barrel and put the other bullet in and snapped the barrel shut.

He gave it a whirl before speaking. "I know what the streets are saying. That's not why I'm here. I want to know who were the three niggas you or Chuka got to murder Henry and his girl."

Supreme was sobbing too loud to hear anything Manny had said.

Paula walked to the head of the bed and caressed his cheek, soothing him some what. "Shh, baby. You need to focus and answer the questions so we can uncuff you and get out of here."

He quieted down and pleaded to her. "Please tell him that I had nothing to do with what happened."

Paula looked toward Manny. "I think he's telling the truth."

Supreme turned to Manny bobbing his head up and down. "On my mother's grave, Manny, I'm telling the truth." Supreme could see the tenseness leaving Manny's body, and he thanked God when Manny put the gun in his coat pocket.

"Paula is a human lie detector," Manny said, "and if she says that you're telling the truth, then I got to go with it."

Supreme swore to himself that he was out of the game for good. No amount of money was worth dying for. And he was going to church with his grandmother every Sunday.

The gleam of something shiny in Paula's hand caught his eye. He turned toward her and saw a straight razor in her hand.

When she saw the panic in his eyes, she put her finger to his lips. "Shh, baby."

Manny used her distraction to reach into the back of his waistband and pull out the other .38, this one had a silencer on it.

When Paula backed away from the bed, Supreme turned back to Manny, only to be staring at the end of a silencer. Manny shot him in the head twice.

Supreme felt two thuds to his head, and then he felt his body go numb. He screamed, but his mouth didn't move. He could faintly hear voices around him. He could barely make them out.

Manny said something about Queens.

The last thing he felt was a tug on his groin, and the last thing he saw was Paula stuffing his severed penis in his mouth.

Chapter 21

Brian's mother woke him up with a smack to the back of his head.

He jumped up disoriented. "C'mon, Ma."

"Get your ass up and get dressed."

Brian held his pounding head. "It's Saturday morning."

"I know what day it is, and if you would've answered your phone last night when I was trying to call you, you would know that you have an interview at the hospital this morning."

"Ahh," Brian groaned. "An interview on a Saturday?"

"The nurse administrator is doing this as a personal favor for me, so she has to do it when she's got the time. The time is this morning. So get up, wash your stinking ass, and let's go; I'm going to be late for work."

Begrudgingly, Brian got up and headed to the bathroom. While in the shower, he tried to piece together what had happened last night in LI. *Those dudes are foul,* he thought. *Selling crack, dope, weed, and whatever else to the adults while they corrupted and fucked their kids.* He thought of Equality banging the life out of Shorty. That's when he remembered that he left his gun at that house. He hoped it would be there when he went back there tonight. He thought about Sonia and her being pregnant. There was no way in hell he could tell his parents. They would freak out. It was bad enough that he and his mother didn't tell his father about Christopher. Now, to just spring this on him and then his son by Denise would be more than enough to put his father over the edge. He thought about the five hundred thousand he'll soon have his hands on. He couldn't wait to get his hands on that money so that Sonia and he could move to Atlanta, Georgia, and start fresh. She could practice law down there, while he runs his internet business from home. He finally focused on the matter at hand, the job interview.

Sonia wanted him to go back to school or get a job; his mother and father wanted him to do something with his life. So getting this job would actually be good for him. He could keep his parents at bay, always wanting to know where he's getting money from to buy clothes, jewelry, a truck, etc., and Sonia would see that he's committed to their relationship. *Fuck it,* he thought to himself. *I'm going to get this job.*

That same morning, Chuka was awakened by his cell phone that wouldn't stop ringing.

He retrieved it from his night stand and answered it. "Hello?"

He was stunned into the upright position when he heard the news coming from the other end of the line. "They found him where?" He looked up to the ceiling and closed his eyes. "Does his grandmother know yet?"

"No," said the voice on the line. "Do you want me to go over there?"

"No. Let the police do it. I want y'all to find out what the fuck happened."

Chapter 22

Brian waited in the lounge for the nurse administrator. He flipped through the magazines that were spread across the waiting area table.

Ten minutes later, he occupied himself by counting the tiles on the floor then the ones on the ceiling. Patience was never one of his virtues.

"I'm going to give this chick ten more minutes, and then I'm out of here," Brian said to himself.

Fifteen minutes later, she walked out of her office.

Brian couldn't believe how young she was. He was expecting an overweight white lady with blotchy skin in her mid fifties.

Instead, he was staring at a twenty-two to twenty-five-year-old caramel-complexioned shorty. Her face was blemish free, eyebrows freshly plucked, lips ripe, and her eyes were so engaging that the rectangular Giorgio Armani glasses they were imprisoned behind couldn't keep Brian from falling under their spell.

As she walked up to him, she kept her clipboard over her chest while she extended her right hand.

Brian stood to greet her.

She shook his hand. "So, you're Brian. Your mom has nothing but good things to say about you."

She had to be five feet four inches, Brian thought. Her nails were manicured, toenails probably pedicured as well. She probably waxed her legs and private area.

He blushed. "Mom gives me more credit than I deserve."

"Well, let's go to my office and get started."

"Sure."

She led the way. She wore a white hospital smock, and as loose as it was, it couldn't hide the assets that God blessed her with.

She walked in and closed the door behind them. "Have a seat." He sat in the seat in front of her desk.

She leaned on the edge of her desk and folded her arms, clipboard covering her chest. "So tell me a little about yourself?"

"Well...uh...my name is Brian, but you know that," he said, cracking a nervous smile. "I graduated high school last year. I'm eighteen years old, and...I'm nervous as hell. Please bear with me."

She smiled. "Relax. You have no reason to be nervous. My name is Marilyn Thomas, I'm twenty-seven years old, and I've been the nurse administrator here at New York Hospital for three years." She lowered her clipboard and flipped through his application. "Everything seems to be in order."

Brian exhaled.

"Except for your answer on question no. 26."

He sighed.

"You checked yes, indicating that you were convicted of a crime, but you left the space blank where you had to explain the offense you were convicted of. You mind sharing it?"

"Well, I was on Far Rockaway beach one night and a friend of mine flashed a gun I never seen one before, so I asked him if I could see it. When he passed it to me, two cops appeared out of nowhere. I had the gun in my possession, so they charged me with it."

Marilyn appeared to be listening intently. "So did you go to prison, or did you get probation?"

"I did eight months on Riker's Island."

"How old were you?"

"I was sixteen going on seventeen, but I lied and told them I was eighteen."

"And you still managed to graduate from high school?"

"I went to night school and summer school."

"So when you fix your mind to do something, you do it?"

"Yes, ma'am."

Ms. Thomas studied him for a moment, a moment that seemed like an eternity.

Finally she spoke. "You present yourself well, and your mother and I are good friends. I need you to understand that if I get you into the janitorial department, you need to take the job seriously, just like you took graduating seriously. Are we clear?"

Did she say janitor? As in swinging a mop and cleaning other people's shit?

A miniature image of his mother and father stood on his left shoulder and Sonia's image on his right.

"Yes, we're clear. Thank you for giving me the opportunity despite my past."

They shook hands, and Brian let himself out.

When he arrived at his mother's workstation, he could only see the top of her head. Files were stacked all around her desk. Meanwhile, the white secretaries were sitting at their desks doing minimal work.

"Ma, why you doing all the work by yourself?" Brian asked loud enough for the rest of the secretaries to hear him.

"Boy, lower your voice. Don't come in here embarrassing me."

"I'm just saying—"

"Don't say anything."

His mother put the folder in her hand down. "So how did it go?"

"I think I got the job," he said, smiling from ear to ear.

"That's good. I'm glad to hear that."

"Ma, Sonia's pregnant."

His mother was speechless.

He surprised himself when he blurted it out. He was never the type to keep secrets from his mother, no matter what it was. Seeing his mother at a loss of words, he tried to help her out.

"Well, aren't you going to say something?"

"I...I don't know what to say."

"I'd rather you curse me out than not say anything."

She picked up some folders and straightened them out. "You're going to have to tell your father. Not just about Sonia, but about Denise and Christopher as well."

"He ain't got to know. Even if I did tell him, all he would do is yell and scream and really want to kick me out."

"That's not the point, Brian. He's your father. He should know."

"You tell him then."

"I'm not the one sticking my dick in women and getting them pregnant." Her face reddened when the rest of the secretaries looked at her.

"Damn, Mom. Why don't you just get on the PA system and tell everybody my business?"

"Brian—"

It was too late. He was out the door.

Chapter 23

On the way home, Brian had worked up the courage to tell his father about this son and about Sonia. He stopped at the corner store and brought a six-pack of Heineken. He felt the tightness leave his body after drinking the third bottle. "It's Saturday afternoon," he said to himself. "What's the chances of him being home anyway?" That wishful thought flew out the window when he saw his father's car parked in the driveway.

As soon as he walked inside, he heard Calypso Rose blaring from the CD player in the living room. He changed his mind. "I'm going straight to my room and lie down for a couple hours," he said to himself.

"Where you coming from?" his father asked. He was sitting on the couch in his underwear, cleaning his service revolver.

So much for going straight to my room. "I just came from an interview at Mom's job."

"You think you got the job?"

"I feel pretty confident about it."

Wow! Brian thought. *We're having a conversation without yelling and screaming.*

Brian tried to slide off on a good note, but he didn't move fast enough.

"Well, I hope you get that job so you can stop selling that crack or weed or whatever it is you're selling."

Weave it, Brian. You knew it was coming.

"I don't sell drugs, Dad. Never have, never will."

"Well, tell me what I got to do to be able to sleep 'til twelve o'clock in the afternoon, then hang out 'til three, four in the morning, and don't have to worry about working because I always have money. Money that I spend on myself, that I don't contribute to the mortgage nor to the food I eat. Please, Brian, enlighten me. Tell me what I got to do."

Bob and weave, baby. You got this.

"All you got to do is get a construction job."

"A construction job, huh?" That's what drug dealers call themselves now, construction workers?"

Enough of the bobbing and weaving.

"If you're so sure that I'm a drug dealer, why don't you arrest me? That's what cops do, right? Y'all still arrest drug dealers, right?"

His father worked the white bristle brush deeper into the nozzle of his gun.

"Boy, you playing a dangerous game," his father said. "You don't want to get me started." He began jamming the bullets back into the gun. "I seen some shit in Vietnam, and I did some shit in Vietnam. Killing comes natural for me."

Brian could see his father working himself up into frenzy. It was time to disappear to his room.

"Boy, I'll take you out. Don't fuck with me, I'll take you out. Post traumatic stress, boy. A jury would find me not guilty. Keep talking to me like I'm one of the niggas in the street."

His father slammed the gun on the coffee table. "Go ahead. Say one more thing. I dare you. Anything. Say it. Ask me what time it is. Ask me what's for dinner."

Brian didn't make any sudden movements. He slowly walked away and headed up to his room.

Chapter 24

Brian walked into Jamaica Hospital looking for Jason and Laquana. He received a voice mail from Jason telling him to get there as soon as possible. Laquana was the first to see him. She ran to him and hugged him. His heart raced when he saw her black eye and busted lip. He hugged her back stiffly. "What's going on? What happened?"

Laquana started crying.

Jason walked up to them and put his hand on her shoulder. "They got robbed in the mall parking lot."

Brian cocked his head.

Jason continued. "Some...girls...a group of girls rolled up on them and started snatching their jewelry. Teshawna started fighting back, so they jumped her, beat her down real bad."

Laquana cried even louder on Brian's chest.

Brian stared at Jason who avoided his eye contact. Brian shook his head.

Laquana looked up at him. "She lost the baby."

"The baby? She was pregnant?"

"Yes, she told me two weeks ago, but she didn't want anybody to know."

Brian cut his eyes at Jason who was now breathing hard. Brian asked the question Jason desperately needed to know the answer to. "Did she tell you who the father...was?"

"No, she didn't want him to be part of their lives. She didn't even tell the bastard."

Jason finally worked up enough courage to look Brian in his eyes. Brian shook his head in disgust.

The whole situation reeked of Jason. When it came to self-preservation, he held no punches or kicks to the stomach for that matter.

Brian sat with them for an hour. They tried to get in to see Teshawna, but she refused to see them. The doctor convinced them that she needed time to grieve her loss.

Brian looked at his watch. He had to go to Long Island to take care of his unfinished business. He kissed Laquana on the forehead and told her he would be over when Teshawna got home to pay her a visit.

When Brian pulled up to the strip bar, he was surprised to see the church next to it open. People were filing in for a Saturday night service. Brian chuckled at the contradiction and the lesson he learned at the same time. The only thing that separates heaven and hell is one step. He parked down the block and headed into the bar. Powerful and the gang sat at their regular table in the back.

Powerful's eyes lit up when he saw him. "Peace, Bee." He slapped him five.

Equality and Knowledge nodded. "Peace to the god."

Brian responded, "Peace."

Equality had a shit-eating grin plastered on his face. Brian felt the blood rushing to his head as his mind flashed back to last night's backroom episode.

Knowledge broke the tension with a question. "So what brings you around, god?"

Brian answered. "I just came to hang out with the gods, see what else y'all do for fun."

All three of them laughed.

"All right," Brian said, "I'm lying. I want to know what's up with this spot Bret is talking about."

They all shook their heads. Equality was the first to speak. "I was wondering when you were going to broach the subject."

"Well, being that tonight seems like a free night, we might as well not let it go to waste."

"Never that, Bee," Powerful said. "None of our nights are wasted. If we ain't fucking, we fucking."

They all laughed at Powerful's corny sense of humor. Brian's smile came as an afterthought.

Equality turned up his bottle of Heineken, polishing it off. "So how about giving us a ride in that Pathfinder of yours?"

"I don't see why not."

Powerful and Knowledge sat in the back while Equality sat up front with Brian, which confirmed his suspicions. Equality was the shot caller. Powerful was the pit bull, and Knowledge's role was yet to be determined.

Equality guided Brian through Hempstead. They drove around talking about the so-called new kid on the block who just made himself at home in Long Island and helped himself to a slice of the pie. A few minutes later, they were parked on a side street. Equality told Brian to cut the engine off. The neighborhood was quieter than a graveyard.

"See the house back there on the left, the white and yellow one?" Equality said.

Brian looked in his rearview mirror. "That's the stash house?"

"That's it. That's the new kid on the block's stash house."

Brian studied the house. He spotted two cameras, one on each corner of the house, which probably meant there were two cameras at the back of the house as well.

"So what are the logistics?" Brian asked.

Knowledge answered. "Everything runs like clockwork. There are three shifts: 7 a.m. to 3 p.m., 3 p.m. to 11 p.m., and 11 p.m. to 7 a.m. There are four men on each shift."

Brian now knew his role.

"Which shift is your man on?"

"The 3 to 11 shift."

Brian's mind was working at the speed of thought. His silence made them fidgety.

Brian addressed Knowledge. "So how are we getting in?"

"That's your area of expertise, right?"

So much for the name Knowledge.

Equality spoke up. "Even with our guy on the inside, that place is still impenetrable. The only time that door opens is for shift change."

Brian smiled. "That's not the only time that door opens."

"What do you mean by that, Bee?" Powerful asked.

"Nothing yet."

They all looked at him puzzled.

"What?" Brian asked.

Then he explained. "The reason why y'all can't see any way in is because you believe there is no way in, so you stifle your mind's creativity. Me, on the other hand, I believe there's a way in, and I believe that shift change isn't the only time that door opens. Those two beliefs are like two sticks. All I got to do is rub them together and viola, I spark my mind's creativity."

Knowledge was the first one to speak. "Did you just call us stupid?"

"No, what I'm saying is y'all are looking at the whole situation wrong. The glass is half full."

Powerful scratched his head. "What glass?"

"Enough of the *Matrix* bullshit," Equality said. "Do you have a way to get in or not?"

"Right now, no."

No one said a word. Brian started the truck. "I'm gonna get back with y'all in a couple days, and trust me, I'll have everything mapped out."

When Brian pulled up in front of the bar, he grabbed Powerful by the arm. "I need to go back to the house we were at last night. I left something in the dresser drawer."

"Damn, Bee. You can't leave anything in a crack head's house, that shit's probably gone by now."

"Hopefully it's not."

Powerful looked at him for a moment then said, "Fuck it, let's go." He told Equality and Knowledge where they were headed and twenty minutes later, they were in front of the house. They both got out of the truck and walked toward the front door.

Powerful turned the knob and just walked in.

The house looked deserted. Empty beer bottles and candy wrappers were sprawled on the floor and all over the tables. The house smelled like wet skunk.

Brian's heart was beating fast. Although this was a crack head's house, it was still someone's house. Someone's house he entered without their permission. *Fuck it,* he thought, *I'm gonna get my gun and I'm out of here.*

He walked to the backroom and opened the door. He was surprised to see Shorty who Equality was jack hammering last night, curled up in the bed. He walked to the dresser and opened the drawer. He let out a sigh when he saw his gun lying on top of a pile of bunched-up panties. He put the gun in his waistband and turned toward Shorty. He walked toward her and bent down next to her. He studied her face, trying to guess her age.

Powerful busted up into the room. "Yo, god."

Brian almost jumped out of his skin.

"You found what you looking for?"

Before Brian could get the words out of his mouth, Powerful was walking over to the bed.

"Aye, Sha-sha, get up." He kicked the bed.

She jumped up disoriented.

"Where's my man's shit at?"

"Yo, P," Brian said, pointing to his waist. "I got it."

"Let's get the hell out of here then."

Sha-sha rubbed her eyes and stared at him, trying to place his face.

"Yo, P. Let's go."

Powerful picked one of her pillows off the floor and threw it at her. "Get your lazy ass out of the bed and clean this place up."

• • •

Devon pulled up to Sunrise Cinemas in his milk white Range Rover. He didn't plan on coming to the movies by himself, but Sharon, his off and-on girl, was on her period and he wasn't taking any woman out who wasn't fucking him that night, period.

He stood on the ticket line and brought his ticket to *Diary of a Mad Black Woman* and then made his way to the concession stand. He cracked a smile at cutie who kept turning around to sneak a peek at him. She blushed and turned back around.

He had on a black denim Nautica suit with a pair of black Timbs. Before he left Sharon's house, he let her grease his dreads and shape up his beard and mustache. The only jewelry he ever wore was a platinum chain with a platinum-diamond-encrusted cross. He didn't believe in the white blue-eyed god black people were indoctrinated to believe in. For him, the cross meant something else. It reminded him of how Jesus was betrayed by one of his own. The cross for him meant "trust no one."

He was surprised to see Shorty standing in line to see the same movie as him. She tried to be discreet, but Devon caught her turning around and staring at him.

He didn't approach her at first. He wanted to see if she was with anyone. When they walked into the movie theatre, he sat next to her. "How you doing?" he asked.

"I'm fine."

"No doubt about that."

Shorty blushed.

Devon continued the conversation. "So you here by yourself?"

"Umm hmm."

"You got a name?"

She answered him while sipping on her soda "Umm hmm."

Mentally, Devon replaced the straw with his dick, and he liked what he saw. Devon was never into foreplay, or any games for that matter. He got right to the point. "I'm jealous."

She looked at him puzzled. "Jealous of what?"

"I wish I was that straw right about now."

Shorty laughed, put her lips back on her straw, and cut her eyes at him before taking another sip.

"So what's your plans for tonight?" he asked.

"I'm gonna watch this movie and then head home."

"How 'bout watching this movie and let me take you to my home?"

"I don't think so. I don't know you like that."

"You will after the movie."

Shorty looked apprehensive. "I don't know about all that."

"I tell you what. After the movie, let me drive you home. If you feel like hanging out, we'll hang out. If not, you hop out and never see me again."

She didn't answer.

"Sounds fair to me, Shorty. So what's up?"

"My name ain't Shorty."

"Pardon me, Shorty. What's your name?"

"My name is Paula."

• • •

Brian called Andrea up on his way back from Long Island. He knew her mother usually worked the night shift on the weekends. "Hey, Ma. What's up?"

"I'm lying in bed waiting for you to come rescue me."

"Your mom is working tonight?"

"She just left. How come you didn't call me back? I left about fifty messages on your voice mail."

Brian shook his head. "How many times do I have to tell you to stop leaving messages on my cell? You know Sonia checks my voice mail. What the fuck is wrong with you?"

Andrea was silent.

"You know what, I'll see you some other time."

"No! Daddy, I'm sorry. I just wanted to talk to you. For now on, if you don't pick up, I won't leave a message."

Brian was silent. He loved it when she begged.

"Daddy, I said I'm sorry. It won't happen again."

Silence.

Brian hung up. Andrea called right back, but he didn't answer.

He turned off Long Island Expressway and headed toward her house. When he turned on to her street, his phone rang. He looked down at the number. It was Sonia.

"What's going on, baby?"

"Nothing. I'm just calling to see what you're up to."

"I'm on my way back from Long Island."

"What's in Long Island?"

"I was celebrating."

"Celebrating?"

"I'm going to be a father, remember?"

"You should be celebrating with me."

Brian thought about the last time he was at her house. "So what's up with your parents?"

"Dad is coming around. Mom is working on him. She can't wait to talk to you."

"Oh yeah?"

"Yeah, she's going to lay down the law on what she's going to expect from you. She said her grandbaby ain't going to be running the streets—like you know who."

Brian laughed. "Your mom is bugged out."

"You know what else is bugged?"

"Nah, baby. What's that?"

She lowered her voice and whispered into the phone. "I'm horny as hell. I've never been this hot in my life."

"Is that so?" Brian said laughing.

"Hell, yeah, but I refuse to play with myself when I got a man to do that."

"So what you saying?"

"Get your ass over her now."

Brian pulled up in front of Andrea's house. Hearing Sonia talk like that had him going. That's the dirtiest she ever spoke to him. For months, he's been trying to get her to accept the nontraditional way of making love. What she called fucking. Sonia believed that only hoes fuck and anything outside of sucking on nipples and missionary style was considered fucking.

Right now, Brian wanted to fuck. He wanted his dick sucked and worshipped. He was at a crossroad.

"Baby, I'll be there in about thirty minutes."

"Thirty minutes? Why so long?"

"I'm on the highway now, baby."

"I don't know if I can wait that long."

Brian couldn't believe what he was hearing. "Damn, baby, you sound like you want to fuck my brains out."

"Don't play yourself, boy," Sonia responded.

She made up his mind for him.

"I'll be there in thirty minutes."

Brian cut off the engine and headed toward Andrea's house. She opened the door before he made it to the top of the steps. She stood by the door wearing a red tank top and a pair of red thongs.

The night breeze had her nipples harder than Brian's dick. She didn't say a word. She opened the screen door and let him in.

Brian walked over to the couch and sat down. He pulled his pants and underwear down and leaned back.

Andrea kneeled in between his legs and began her worship.

• • •

Devon walked hand in hand with Paula to his truck. She couldn't stop laughing or talking about the movie.

"That was the funniest movie I ever seen in my life," she said.

"It was all right."

"All right? It was off the chain." Paula kept laughing so she could hide her fear.

When she first laid eyes on him from the back of Manny's BMW, shivers ran up and down her spine. His walk was confident yet light. When he sat next to her in the movie theatre, he greeted her with the smile of an angel and analyzed her with the eyes of a shark. Now she was walking with him to his truck, formulating a plan on how to get him to the hotel where Jennifer and Manny were lying in ambush.

Devon opened the door for her to get in.

He's a gentleman, she thought to herself. *Until he palmed her butt.* She jumped but tried to recover by slapping his hand.

"Boy, you scared me."

He just smiled and walked to the driver's side.

Devon hopped in and popped in his John Legend CD. "So where we headed to, Shorty—I mean, Paula?"

"I thought you were running the show."

Devon grinned. "I'm driving, but you're in control."

Paula looked at him with a devilish grin. "Well, the Holiday Inn sounds good."

Ten minutes later, Devon turned on Baisley Boulevard, away from the Holiday Inn. He pulled up into Baisley Park.

Paula looked around with a nervous smile. "Why we stopping here?"

"We're here."

"Where's here."

"The Holiday Inn," Devon said reaching into his armrest and pulling out a condom.

"Maybe you should take me home."

"Home?"

Devon slapped her.

Paula was in shock.

"Listen, Shorty, you got two choices. Make believe I'm that straw you were so seductively sucking on, or you can get out right here."

Paula's eyes welled with tears. She swept her hair behind her ears and held her hand out for the condom.

Devon grinned as he handed it to her and said, "Cool."

• • •

Andrea swallowed every drop of Brian before she looked up at him.

He opened his eyes and said, "Stand up." He motioned for her to take off her tank top. He kissed her stomach, then pulled her thong down and watched her step out of it. He turned her around and slapped her hard on the butt.

She jumped.

He pulled her down by the hips until he buried his stallion deep into her stable.

She let out a small cry when he grabbed her by the hair and yanked her head back. She arched her back, releasing some of the tension on her hair and allowing him to bury himself all the way to the tilt. She rode him until he exploded deep inside of her.

Brian looked at his watch and cursed under his breath. "Baby, I gotta go."

"What? You just got here."

"I got a couple more stops to make."

Andrea got off of him, picked up her underwear and tank top off the floor, and stormed upstairs.

Brian went into the bathroom and washed up. He thought about going upstairs to talk to her, but said fuck it. She'll get over it. She always does. He hopped into his truck and wasn't surprised to hear his phone ringing. He answered it. "Sonia, I'm ten minutes away."

"I'll be outside waiting for you." She hung up.

Brian was huffing. He was still in animal mode. He pictured bending Sonia over the passenger seat and just drilling her from behind. He erased that thought from his mind. That will never happen, not even in his wildest dreams.

He pulled up surprised to see her in her pastel mink jacket, miniskirt, and high heels.

She climbed in and kissed him long and hard.

"Damn, baby. Why you all dressed up?"

"I can't look sexy for my man?"

"Sure you can, but you're a mother now, you can't be dressing like that. What would our unborn child think?"

"Shut up, Brian."

Sonia was in heat. Brian could feel the fire radiating off of her. "Take off that hot ass jacket. It's making me hot."

Sonia unzipped her jacket. Brian swerved.

He was staring at her bare chest. "You need to get pregnant more often."

They both laughed.

"Turn right here," Sonia said, pointing down a side street. Brian turned down the street.

"Park right here," she said.

Brian parked in front of a green-and-white house. "Who lives here?"

"I don't know."

"So why you told me to park here?"

She grabbed his hand and put it under her skirt.

Brian felt no panties. All he felt was a swollen clit.

She cut him off before he got his words out. "I always wanted to do it outdoors."

While she was living out her fantasy, Brian was fighting a Dr. Jekyll-and-Mr.-Hyde war within, and he was losing. He wanted to rip her skirt off, put her legs on his shoulders, and plow deep inside her.

He played with her clit as she unbuttoned his pants and freed willy. He closed his eyes and stifled a growl. He opened his eyes, and the first thing he saw was Sonia licking her lips and looking down at his manhood. Mr. Hyde broke loose.

Sonia was shocked at the speed Brian hopped over to the passenger seat, let it down, and turned her over on her stomach.

He pulled her to her knees, and before she could protest, he lifted her skirt and plunged his magic stick deep inside her.

She tried to squirm away from him, but he was on her like glue. "Brian, stop! Brian, get off!" she screamed.

Mr. Hyde grunted with each thrust.

"Brian!" Sonia screamed. "No!...Please...don't stop."

• • •

Devon smiled from ear to ear when Paula tore the condom open. His smile broadened when she wiped the tears from her eyes. When she reached for his zipper, he stopped her.

She looked at him confused.

"I'm just fucking with you, Shorty."

Paula exhaled.

Devon reached into his glove compartment and pulled out a pair of handcuffs. "You can put these on though."

Paula cocked her head.

Devon punched her in the head. "This time, I'm not fucking with you, Shorty. Put them on."

Paula put the cuffs on.

Devon searched her bag. No wallet, no ID, all he found was a straight razor and cell phone. "So who's waiting for us at the Holiday Inn, Shorty?"

"Nobody is waiting for—"

Devon punched her in the head again.

Paula started shaking. "You're crazy. I swear. There's no one waiting for us. I just want to go home. Please take me home."

• • •

Brian couldn't believe what was happening. He was fucking the shit out of Sonia from behind, and she begged him not to stop.

Mrs. Hyde was too much for him, he exploded into her.

Sonia finally squirmed from under him and turned on her back. She stared at him for a second then slapped him hard.

"Don't you ever manhandle me like that again." She smirked.

In one fluid motion, Brian cocked her legs on his shoulders and plunged back into her.

Sonia protested with a groan.

• • •

"This is your last chance, Shorty. Who's at the hotel?"

Paula's dam of tears broke.

Devon studied her for a moment, then reached into the glove compartment and retrieved the hand-cuff key.

"Listen, Shorty," Devon said, "women, decent women never offer to go to a hotel with a man they don't know. I didn't even tell you my name, and you're ready to go to a hotel with me? So you got to understand why I got a little paranoid, you dig?"

Paula nodded weakly.

Devon uncuffed her then reached past her and opened the door. "Get out."

Paula was stunned.

When he cocked his fist back, she jumped out the truck.

Paula pleaded with him. "Can I have my phone to call a cab?"

"There's a pay phone next to the school over there." He threw four quarters at her before pulling off.

Paula's crocodile tears dried up immediately as she ran to the pay phone. "The paranoid motherfucker knew," she said into the phone. Manny was silent. He handed the phone to Jennifer.

"Are you all right?"

"I got a massive headache."

"Where you at?"

"Across from Baisley Park, next to August Martin High School."

"We're on our way."

Devon had doubled back and was looking at Paula through his high-powered binoculars. She just got off the phone and was just standing there with her arms folded across her chest.

The Holiday Inn was right across from JFK airport, so whoever she called would be there in about fifteen minutes.

He got out his truck with his six-shot .44 mag in hand. He inched closer, using the trees to camouflage his approach. He now stood sixty feet away. Far enough to be out of sight, close enough to line her up in his. *I'll pop the driver first,* he thought. *Then whoever's in the car, then her.* He calmed his breathing. In about five minutes, it was going to be the Fourth of July.

• • •

Sonia lay on Brian's chest, fast asleep. He couldn't believe tonight's episode. *What else would she be open to if I pressed her?* he thought. *Here we are butt naked, parked in the street where anyone can walk up on us, and she's sound asleep.* Brian fell in love with her all over again. He was even considering ending it with Andrea. After all, if he could get everything from one woman, why have two?

His mind drifted to LI. He knew exactly how he was going to get the loot and the drugs—that wasn't the problem. The problem was avoiding a bullet to the back of the head from Equality, Knowledge, or

Powerful. Money and drugs have a way of making a motherfucker greedy.

When he made the deal with Bret, he knew Bret was talking out his ass. There was no way that them LI cats were going to let him walk away with half a million dollars and over fifty kilos of coke. *Three years,* Brian thought. *Doing Bret's dirty work for over three years and just like that, I become expendable. Maybe Bret panicked. Maybe he thought Tequan would find out somehow that he had something to do with one of his lieutenant's getting robbed and murdered. Maybe he's giving him an offering. He gets fifty kilos, the LI cats get half a million, and Tequan gets a life for a life. So everybody comes out a winner, except yours truly. Question: How do I get the money, the drugs, and at the same time get rid of Bret and the LI cats—permanently?* Brian's mind kicked in to overdrive.

●   ●   ●

Finally, the 745Li BMW pulled up alongside the phone booth. Instead of raising his gun, Devon raised his phone and hit speed dial.

"What up, nigga?" Brian whispered into the phone, so not to wake Sonia up. "You must be in some shit because you never call me."

"Bitch tried to set me up tonight."

Brian laughed. "What else is new, nigga? You live for that shit."

"Manny sent her."

Brian shot up, waking Sonia out of her sleep. "Where you at?"

"Baisley Park, watching her hop into his ride."

"You can see them?"

"Clear as day."

Brian knew what he meant. "Let them go."

Devon lowered the .44 mag back to his side. "So what's the plan?"

"We gonna pay Tequan a visit."

Devon nodded. "Cool."

Chapter 25

Brian was the first one to pull up to the schoolyard. He hopped out of his Pathfinder with two Heinekens in his hand and walked into the yard.

A few minutes later, Jason and Devon pulled up from opposite sides of the street. When Jason got in smacking distance, Brian swung at him.

"Aye, yo, Bee. What up?"

"What you think is up? Why you get them bitches to jump Teshawna and Laquana?"

"C'mon, Bee. That bitch was trying to play me."

"So you get her beat the fuck up and let your girl get jumped in the process?"

"I told them not to give it to her too bad, just make it look good."

Devon shook his head. "That's cold blooded, Jay."

"Fuck that," Jason said. "And if I even think that she's going to tell Laquana, I'll kill her myself."

"She lost the baby, Jay," Brian said. "You're going to burn in hell for that."

"Fuck that. God knows what my intentions were."

Devon changed the subject. "So what are we going to do with this Manny situation?"

Jason nodded in agreement.

"Okay," Brian said. "Tell us what happened last night from the beginning."

Devon told them from the time he first saw Shorty clocking him up to Manny pulling up to get her.

Brian and Jason listened attentively.

"Why would they come after you?" Brian asked.

They all thought the obvious, but Jason said it.

"Fucking Bret snitched us out."

"Let's not jump to conclusions," Brian said.

Devon spoke up, "He's not jumping to conclusions. It's obvious."

"Well," Brian said, "y'all been in the game just as long as me so y'all should know that nothing in this game is obvious."

"So back to the original question. What are we going to do?" Jason asked.

"Why don't we just give him a call?" Devon asked.

"Bright idea, Sherlock," Brian said. "Only we don't have his number." Devon held up Paula's cell phone and smiled. Brian and Jason smiled along with him.

Manny picked up on the fifth ring. "What took you so long?"

"What did you want with my boy?" Brian asked.

"I wanted to ask him a few questions."

"You could have done that in person. Why send a chick?"

"I knew he wouldn't let me get within twenty feet of him, so I figured my girl could've established some trust between us."

"You're full of shit, Manny."

"Forget about him. I'm talking to you. What happened last Saturday night?"

"From what I heard, your boy got popped in front of Tequan's building."

"Fuck what you heard! Why'd you do it?" Manny screamed into the phone.

"Hold on playa—"

"No! You hold on, youngin'. I don't know who you think you messing with, but I was in this game when you were still in your daddy's nut sack. You should have enough street smarts to know that for the right price, even the dead will talk. No more talking, youngin'. The next time you see me, you'll be taking your last breath."

Click!

Brian stared at the phone like it tried to bite his ear off. "The motherfucker hung up on me."

"That's not good," Jason said.

• • •

Bret went sailing over the dining room table. As he stumbled to his feet, Devon punched him in the throat and shoved him into the wall.

Jason struggled to restrain Trish as she screamed hysterically.

"Take her upstairs!" Brian shouted.

Jason carried her out, kicking and screaming.

He walked over to Bret and stood over him. "Why'd you rat us out?"

"Bee, you know I wouldn't—"

Devon cut him off with a stiff right to the jaw.

Bret tried to summon up some courage. "You're making a big mistake, Bee!"

"No, you made the mistake. You think I'm scared of you. You think I won't put two in you and then go put two in Trish?"

If fear ever had a face, it was Bret's.

Devon picked him up by his collar and sat him down on one of the dining room chairs.

Brian grabbed one of the overturned chairs and sat in front of him. "Manny knows that we pulled that robbery last Saturday, Bret."

Bret was breathing hard and rubbing his jaw. "It wasn't me."

"The only ones who knew about it were you, me, Dev, and Jay. No one else."

Bret cut his eyes at Devon. "How you know it wasn't one of them?"

Devon punched him in the back of the head. When his head snapped back up, Brian punched him in the front.

"Don't ever disrespect my team. We go way back."

Bret spoke through swollen lips. "We go way back too."

"No doubt. All the way back to taking your lunch money and giving you wedgies."

Brian stared at him. Bret knew that look all too well. "You don't have to do this, Bee."

"Do what, Bret? What am I going to do?"

Bret's words got caught up in his tears.

Brian pulled out the Glock and put it to Bret's head.

Bret kept shaking his head and mouthing, "It wasn't me."

Fuck, Brian thought. *What if it wasn't him? If I kill him, I'm gonna have to kill Trish as well. Three bodies in one week. Fuck! Think. How can I prove that it was him or not him?*

His mind sparked. He turned to Devon. "Go get me the house phone."

Manny picked up on the fifth ring. "Since when do you call me, Bret?"

"I just got off the phone with Bee, and he says that you think he did that thing last Saturday night."

"What's wrong with your voice?"

Bret looked up at Brian listening on the other line as if he was waiting for him to give him an answer.

Manny continued. "You sound fucked up. You high, nigga?"

"Nah...I'm just getting my head right, you know?"

"Nah, nigga. I don't know. You strung out on your own shit."

Brian and Devon looked at each other.

Bret changed the subject. "How'd you figure Bee and them had something to do with that?"

"I got my sources, nigga."

"Well...I got my sources too."

"And?"

"And I know they didn't do it."

Manny was silent for a moment. "So who did, Bret?"

"I don't know, but I know it wasn't them. I got Bee doing something for me in LI. So I know he ain't have nothing to do with that."

"What is he doing in LI?"

"Casing out a spot."

Manny was at the end of his patience. "Why you trying to cover for that nigga? Let me tell you something." Manny said emphasizing every word. "At first, you were gonna get it too, but when I found out that he did this behind your back, I decided to let you live."

Brian's face was wrinkled in confusion.

"Now, you know how Tequan is." Manny let the implication set in. "Consider yourself lucky."

"Your info is wrong," Bret said weakly.

Manny laughed loud enough for the dead to hear. "Nigga! I'm never wrong!"

Manny hung up. Brian held the other phone in his hand. Devon looked at him, waiting for the next move. Brian just stared at him. For the first time in his life, Brian was brain locked.

"Jay," Brian yelled, "get down here!"

Brian had butterflies in his stomach, a feeling he hadn't felt since his first robbery. He was at war with the one everybody in the streets called "Maniac Manny." The horror stories about him reached far and wide. He was a behind-the-scenes enforcer with a web of contacts that stretched out over all five boroughs. That's what shook Brian up the most. Manny sounded too confident when he said he was never wrong. He emphasized the *never* as if he knew that he was on the other end listening in on the conversation.

When Jason came down, Trish broke free from him and ran to her brother. She hugged him and let her tears fall on his head as if they would heal his wounds.

Without warning, she charged at Brian and clawed and scratched him. When Brian grabbed her by the wrists, she kicked and spat at him.

Devon ran up behind her and snatched her by her hair and yanked her back to her brother who grabbed her by the waist.

"I hate you!" she spat at Brian, foaming at the mouth.

Her words were like a pair of vice grips clasped around his body, squeezing the life out of him.

Brian knew what he had to do.

"So where do we go from here, Bret?" Brian asked him.

"It's your call," Brian said. "Make it, or I'll make it for us."

Bret said nothing.

"Bret," Brian lowered his voice, "don't make me do this."

Bret didn't respond.

Brian looked at Devon and Jason. "Break out. I'll meet y'all in the truck."

Neither of them moved.

"I said break out!"

Devon was the first to head toward the front door. Jason turned to leave when he heard Devon open the screen door.

Bret pushed his sister away from him. "Get out of here."

Trish's eyes welled with fear; she understood what was about to happen. "No!" she hugged him, using herself as a shield between him and Brian.

He pushed her away again. "Get the fuck out of here!"

Trish fell to her knees and hugged his leg and kept shaking her head. "I'm not leaving."

Bret stood up and slapped her. "You stupid bitch." He slapped her again, then picked her up and pushed her toward the door.

Brian raised out the Glock. "You know I can't let her leave, Bret."

Trish froze.

"You're a lot of things, but a baby killer isn't one of them."

Brian turned the gun on her. "Then you don't know me very well."

Bret looked at Trish. "Turn around and walk out the door, baby."

Trish looked at him then back to Brian.

"Get back over there with your brother."

"Trish, listen to me," Bret said, "turn around and walk out."

He looked at Brian. "If you're going to shoot her, shoot her in the back."

Brian looked at Trish.

"That girl's feelings for you run deep, Bee," Bret said.

"Been in love with you ever since she was in the fourth grade and we were in the sixth. She used to sit right there at the living room window and draw us playing stickball. Your picture always had a heart over it. Remember those days, Bee?"

The Trish staring at him in fear was the fourth grader with the pigtails and glasses.

Bret laughed. "I remember one day the mail-man asked her who she wanted to be when she grew up, and she said Brian's wife. Remember that Trish?"

Trish looked at him and then back to Brian.

"She loves you so much that she gave her virginity to you."

They both looked at him.

He laughed. "What? You think I didn't know?

"I know all about the nights she used to sneak out to get her some Brian."

Bret's voice turned harsh as he looked at Trish. "Turn your ass around and walk out of here."

Trish turned around and took a step.

"Keep going, he ain't gonna shoot."

Bret looked at him. "She's sixteen, Bee, a baby."

Trish looked back at Brian and took another step. She must have seen something in his face because her steps grew a little more confident.

She turned the knob and ran out into the backyard, toward the alley.

Brian aimed the gun at Bret and pulled the trigger.

Bret jumped when he heard the click.

"Nigga, stop playing."

"Stop crying, it ain't even loaded."

Bret rubbed his head. "Nigga, you said you was gonna make it look real."

"Did it look real?"

"Look at my face, motherfucker. These are real bruises; this is real blood."

"At least you're alive to complain about some bullshit bruises and a little blood."

Brian put the gun back in his waistband. There was an awkward moment between them.

Brian stuck his hands in his pants pockets. "Hey, about Trish and I...."

Bret dismissed it with a wave of his hand. "Trish is old enough to fuck who she wants. So drop it."

"I just want you to know—"

"Nigga, I ain't trying to dwell on the subject. I said it's dead, so let's move on." Bret looked outside the dining room window at Devon and Jason who were sitting in Brian's Pathfinder.

"So which one of your boys snaked you?"

Brian joined him at the window. "I have no fucking idea."

Brian jumped into the truck and peeled off without a word. When he got to a stop light, Devon broke the silence.

"You let him live?"

"He didn't rat us out."

The silence was incriminating.

"You do know what you're saying, right?" Jason said. "The only ones outside of Bret who knew anything about the job are sitting in this truck." Brian kept his eyes on the road.

Devon kept his eyes on him. "I don't like where this is going."

"It ain't going anywhere," Brian said. "We all know that we can't listen to Mr. Always-Jumping-to-Conclusions in the backseat. It all makes sense if you step back and look at it."

Devon and Jason were both lost.

Brian explained. "Think about it, Manny sends a chick at Dev. What happened last Friday night?"

"Supreme," Devon said, hitting himself in the head. "It was all in the papers. They found him in a hotel room." He thought of the chick who called herself Paula trying to get him to the Holiday Inn. "Shot twice in the head."

Jason cut in. "And they said they found his dick in his mouth."

"That wasn't in the paper," Devon said.

"That don't mean it ain't true."

Brian cut them both off. "There's no doubt that was Manny's work.

"Supreme is—was Chuka's right hand. The same Chuka that the lieutenant picked up ten thousand from the same night he picked up the Gs from Bret."

They were all on the same page.

Brian continued. "He tortured that nigga 'til he believed he had nothing to do with it."

"So that only leaves us," Jason said.

"Cause we're the only ones stupid enough to pull some shit off like that," Devon said.

"I prefer crazy enough to pull some shit off like that," Brian said.

"Then there's a thin line between stupid and crazy," Devon said.

"But how did he know where to find Dev?" Jason said.

"Fuck that," Brian said, "that's irrelevant. What we should be focusing on is how do we get rid of this motherfucker before he tries to get rid of us. I don't know about y'all, but I ain't never been the type to sit on my ass and just let a nigga do something to me. We need to bring it to this nigga tonight."

Devon nodded. "Cool."

Chapter 26

Brian stopped at Andrea's to strap up. When she let him in, she noticed Jason and Devon sitting in his truck. Without a word, she followed him upstairs. She leaned against the threshold of her bedroom and watched him open his trunk.

Brian reached in and pulled out his baby—sixteen-shot, .45 cal. a.k.a. fo'fif, or as he lovingly named her, Fifi. He stuck the three clips in his pocket and grabbed the two extra clips he had for the Glock. He reached in the trunk again and pulled out his bulletproof vest. He took off his jacket and put the vest on. He locked the trunk, stood up, and put his jacket back on.

He looked in the mirror to see if his jacket concealed the vest. Then he looked at Andrea.

She refused to look at him. It was her way of disapproving of what he called "doing what I got to do." She folded her arms across her chest and continued looking at the ground.

He slowly walked up to her and stared at her.

She kept her gaze on the ground. He lowered his head to kiss her. She turned the other way. He kissed her on her neck. She pulled away from him. He stroked her hair away from her face and saw the tears in her eyes. He hugged her and let her cry on his vest.

She held on to him, even as he tried to pull away from her. He let his hands fall to the side, but she refused to let him go. At that moment, Brian felt like shit. Despite whatever issues she may have, she was a good girl, Brian thought, *She does anything I want her to do.*

He thought back to that night on Far Rockaway Beach. He knew every time he went out there, there was always one nigga who couldn't keep his mouth shut. His boys from Edgemere projects told him the nigga was all talk and no walk, but he had Andrea with him, and it was the first time he took her somewhere with him. How would he look in her eyes if he just let this nigga pop shit and didn't check him? So checked him he did.

He got up in dude's face and shut it for him. Then scrams made the biggest mistake in his life. He told Brian that he'll be back; if he was still there, he was going to fill him with lead.

Andrea was packing his .25 automatic in her purse. When she heard the threat, she pulled out the .25 and started firing.

Everybody hit the ground, including Brian.

119

Andrea didn't hit scrams with the first three shots, but she steadily walked up to him, ensuring that she wouldn't miss with the next three.

Brian jumped up and ran toward her. He grabbed the gun with one hand and grabbed her by the waist with the other.

"You don't ever threaten my man, nigga. I will fucking kill you!" she screamed.

Scrams got up off the ground and hauled ass.

"What the fuck is wrong with you, girl?" Brian asked shocked.

"Fuck that nigga. I'll kill his fucking ass," she mumbled.

She was scorching.

From that night, he feared her in an erotic kind of way. He felt like a pyromaniac, and she was the fire. Her sniffles brought him back to the present. He grabbed her by the arms and pulled away from her. He headed downstairs and out the door without looking back.

• • •

Brian sat in the back of the stolen Acura, Jason on the driver's side, and Devon on the passenger side.

Being parked half a block down from Tequan's brownstone was like déjà vu.

They sat in silence.

Earlier Devon just wanted to kick the door in and blast everybody. That was the typical Devon's response. Brian didn't like walking into anything blindly. For all he knew, they could've kicked in the door and had machine guns pointed at them.

Jason was the first to notice that Tequan's car wasn't parked anywhere on the block, which probably meant he wasn't home. So he suggested that they just wait for him and Manny to pull up and blast them right there before they stepped out the car.

That sounded good to Brian. Devon preferred his plan though. Jason was the first one to see Tequan's car past them.

"Yo, there he go," he said, tapping the seat.

Jason was out the car, trotting down the block before Brian or Devon reached for their door handles.

Jason heard the car cut off, but no one got out.

They ain't even gonna see it coming, he thought to himself.

Brian and Devon trailed behind.

So far, so good, Devon thought to himself.

This shit is too easy, Brian thought to himself.

When Jason got two cars away, he noticed that neither Tequan nor Manny got out of the car.

Brian's hood sense started tingling. Something was wrong.

It was too easy. It was quiet, too quiet. And as if on cue, he caught a shadowed figure out his peripheral, a shadow with a gun.

Before he could warn Jason, the figure fired.

Jason went down, and Devon fired at the figure. The shadow ducked back in the building he crept out of.

Brian caught up to Jason who was rolling on the ground. "The punk motherfucker shot me, Bee."

Brian looked down at Jason's bloody jacket.

"Nigga, why you ain't got your vest on?"

"That shit...too fucking...bulky," Jason said, grimacing.

Devon continued running toward Tequan's car, shooting out the back windshield. Bullets whizzed by his head from across the street.

Brian now knew that they had walked into the very same thing he wanted to avoid, a trap.

Brian shot at the person shooting at Devon from across the street. A bullet ricocheted inches from his feet. He looked up at Tequan's window where the bullet came from.

"Yeah, motherfucker. You dead motherfucker!" Tequan's next bullet hit Jason in the leg.

"Ah! Fucking bitch!" Jason grabbed his leg.

Brian jumped back and fired up at the window.

"Jay, you got to get back to the car."

Jason didn't hear a word he said. He was in too much agony.

Devon was pinned behind a car by the two guys who hopped out of Tequan's car with UZIs. The hooded figure crept out the building and started shooting at Brian and Jason.

Fuck, this motherfucker is between us and the car, Brian thought. He pulled out Fifi and let her bark. When she exploded, it seemed like every gun jammed out of respect, because for a second, not one shot was fired. When she barked at the figure now hightailing it back into the brownstone, he dropped his gun before diving back into the building. That pause gave Devon enough time to reload and retreat back to where Jason lay. He picked him up and ran with him to the car, while Brian let Fifi loose on the two who were now pinned behind Tequan's car. He fired two shots at Tequan's window and two more shots at the other gunman across the street.

When they got back to the car, Devon noticed the flat tires. "The motherfuckers shot out the tires, Bee."

Tequan, Manny, and the three gunmen were creeping up the block with guns in hand.

"We got to get the fuck out of here," Jason said, wincing.

Brian barked two more shots in Tequan's direction. They flinched, but they kept coming.

Brian thanked God when he heard and saw police sirens coming up from behind Tequan and his boys.

"Yo, Bee," Devon said, "we got to get out of here."

"Get out of here," Jason said.

"We're not just gonna leave you here," Brian said.

"Motherfucker, we no good to each other if we all in prison. I'll just tell them these motherfuckers were trying to rob me."

Devon put Jason down on the ground and looked at Brian.

"Fuck it," Brian said. "Give me your gun."

Jason gave him his gun and the extra clips he had in his pocket.

When Brian saw Tequan and his posse duck into one of the brownstones, he took off with Devon down the block, leaving Jason propped up against a No Parking sign.

When Brian and Devon made it to their rendez-vous spot behind the gas station, Brian's eyes almost popped out of his head when he saw the bullet holes in Devon's vest and the bullet hole in his arm.

"Damn, Dev. Why didn't you say anything?"

"I'm all right, Bee."

"You got a fucking hole in your arm."

"Bullet went clean through."

Devon took off his vest, and Brian saw the red welt marks on his chest and stomach from the impact of the bullets.

"You sure you all right?"

"I'm cool."

Brian still had the shakes and felt safe keeping his vest on. He just hopped into his truck and waited for Devon to get in.

When Brian pulled up in front of his house, he took a deep breath to calm himself down. He knew that nine times out of ten, his mother or father will be up and ready to give him the business. He took off his vest and put it along with his guns in his brown duffle bag.

He threw the bag in the trunk and headed inside.

His mother was waiting at the table for him.

"This is going to be the last time you bring your sorry ass in this house at two in the morning."

"Yeah, Ma. The last time."

"That's right, boy," she said. "Because you can't be getting in at two and expecting to be to work at six."

Brian cocked his head.

His mother was smiling from ear to ear. "You got the job. You start next week Monday morning."

Chapter 27

Brian slept so hard that when he heard ringing in his ears, he woke up, reaching for the alarm clock. He hit it, but the ringing wouldn't stop. He finally realized that it was his cell phone.

He dug into his pants that were crumpled up on the floor and pulled it out. "What?"

"Aye, yo, Bee. "Y'all niggas is crazy," Bret said.

Brian looked at his alarm clock. "It's 7:30 in the morning."

"Well, while you're sleeping, the streets are on fire."

Brian thought back to last night's scene, and all he could think of was leaving Jason behind. As soon as he made it up to his room last night, he called Laquana and told her that he had gotten a call that Jason had been shot in Brooklyn. After five minutes of calming her down and swearing that he didn't know why Jason was in Brooklyn, he told her to call all the hospitals in that area and find out his condition. What he really wanted to know was did the cops arrest him or not. Laquana hadn't called him back yet.

"On fire about what?"

"Nigga, you know."

"Yeah, whatever."

"Manny called me."

Brian's ears perked up. "Oh, yeah?"

"Yeah, he said he wants to talk."

Brian's whole body smiled. "Talk about what?"

"He says too much blood has been shed over this shit and somebody has got to be the bigger man. He wants to be the bigger man."

"How does Tequan feel about him being the bigger man?"

"Nigga, you know Tequan ain't got no say."

"Since when?"

"Since he's laying up in the hospital half past dead."

"What?" Brian fell out the bed.

"What the fuck is wrong with you?" Bret asked.

Brian grabbed his pants and boots and started getting dressed. *What the fuck was going on? Maybe the police chased him down into the building, and he didn't want to give up.*

"What happened? How do you know he's in the hospital, half dead?"

"Nigga, I told you, the streets are on fire. Niggas couldn't wait to call me up and tell me. The shotgun blast did it."

Shotgun blast? Brian thought to himself.

"Hit that nigga twice, Bee. I'm surprised that nigga still alive." Brian's body started to shake, and his hands got sweaty.

"Yo, Bret, I got to call you back."

"Yeah, no doubt."

"Yo," Brian said at the last moment, "you explained to Trish why we had to do that?"

"Nigga, don't even sweat that. She still loves you. She said she never wants to see you again, but she was never a good liar."

Brian laughed. "I'm out, peace."

As soon as he hung up, his phone rang. It was Devon.

"Dev, what up?"

"Meet me at the park."

Click!

Brian didn't have to meet up with Devon to know what had happened. The call said it all.

• • •

Brian sat on the bench in the schoolyard, puffing on a Newport. One could tell when he was nervous because he would get the shakes. So to maintain his cooler-than-ice appearance, he would smoke a cigarette. He took one last pull before he plucked it to the ground and lit another one. He looked at his watch, 11:45 a.m. If it wasn't the summer vacation, the kids would be on their way to the yard for recess.

The only one left in the park was a hottie whom he called Sexy Mama, never to her face though. She was twenty-seven years old with a body that made any woman in her circumference feel insecure. She was playing with her six-year-old son on the monkey bars. Not only did she have the body, she had the brains as well. He couldn't understand how a dude could be blessed to share the same bed with her, knock her up, and then leave her. The exuberance emanating from her soul told one that she didn't need any man or baby daddy to validate her or her life.

She was her own woman and had no problem dealing with her past decisions, good or bad.

Hottie caught him looking at her. She waved.

He waved more so out of embarrassment. *I hope she didn't catch me staring at her ass,* he thought to himself.

She bent down and whispered something to her little man.

Her son looked his way and gave him a sketchy wave then turned his attention back to the monkey bars.

Brian waved back, then looked at his watch. He opened his cell phone and called Devon.

"Yo, where the fuck you at?"

"I'm right behind you."

Brian turned around and saw Devon's Range Rover at the stop light. He mashed his cigarette out when Devon pulled up to the curb.

Brian tired to read Devon's face when he hopped out the truck, but as usual, attempting to read Devon's face was like a blind man trying to read lips.

Brian slapped him five, "What up, nigga?"

"Everything's cool."

"What the fuck happened?"

Devon scanned the park. After registering the hottie and her son as harmless, he took a step closer to Brian. "I was on my way home last night, and I couldn't get Jay out of my mind. You know, the way we just left him there, all shot up."

Devon cut his eyes at hottie. He must have thought she could somehow hear him from way across the park because he leaned into Brian and whispered. "So I went back."

"You went back without me!"

Devon cut his eyes at hottie. Brian looked at her, now he was paranoid. He whispered, "You went back without me?"

"Jay was right. It didn't make sense for all of us to get caught. We won't be good to each other if we all get knocked."

Brian shook his head, but Devon continued.

"When I got back, I spotted two detective cars parked on the block. The ambulance had already taken Jay away. Did you get any word on his condition?"

Brian shook his head. "Nah, I had Laquana calling all night. No hospital has him under his real name. She even used his aliases, but no luck."

"Well, I decided to hang around, see what was up," Devon continued. "The detectives left about three hours later." Devon licked his lips. "Just before sunrise, guess who has the balls to come outside and run to the store?"

"Tequan," Brian answered.

"Mothefucking Tequan," Devon said right back at him.

"Without Manny?"

"Without Manny," Devon said with a smile creeping on his face.

"What did you do?"

"I called you, Bee, but you didn't answer your cell. So I had to take advantage of the situation. I pulled out the pump shotgun and ran up behind him and let him have it." The smile was now apparent on Devon's face. "I hit him twice."

"Well, you should've hit him three times."

Devon looked at him confused.

"The nigga didn't die."

"What the fuck are you talking about?"

"Bret called me this morning right before you did. Manny wants a truce. He said Tequan is in the hospital in critical condition."

"That's impossible!" Devon didn't care who heard him. "That nigga is dead. He had two cannonball holes in his back."

"Well, Manny said—"

"Fuck what Manny said! What did I just say?"

"Whoa, slow your roll, nigga. I'm just relaying to you what was told to me."

"Yeah, well, I was there, so I'm telling you what I saw with my own two eyes. God himself couldn't bring that nigga back to life."

"All right, nigga. I believe you. Manny is probably just trying to keep it under wraps."

Brian's phone rang. "What up, Bret?"

Brian listened to what he had to say without interrupting him. "See you then."

Brian hung up and put his phone away. "Bret set up a meeting with Manny."

"Where?"

"Green Acres Mall."

"Familiar territory," Devon said, nodding his head.

"Familiar, but dangerous," Brian responded. "If anything goes down and we get arrested in Nassau County, it's lights out."

Devon smiled. "Manny's crazy, not stupid."

"There's a thin line between crazy and stupid."

Devon put his palms together. "Let's pray that he doesn't cross the line then."

Brian lit up another cigarette. "I got that job at the hospital."

"Get the fuck out of here."

"Yeah, it's official, I'm gonna be a working stiff."

They both laughed.

Devon got serious for a moment. "What's up with the LI job?"

"I don't know. Jay might not be up to snuff, and we can't do it without him."

Devon thought for a moment. "We can get someone to take his place."

"Absolutely not. Either we're all in it or it's a no
go."

Brian still couldn't decide which one of his boys
sold him out.

Devon definitely proved his loyalty time and time
again, but so did Jason. Maybe it wasn't any of them.
He couldn't take that chance. He knew the game all
too well. Most of the dudes who were murdered in
the game were done in by those closest to them.

"Keep your enemies close, but keep your friends
closer" is what Gritty used to always say.

Gritty was always quoting some philosophical art
of war bullshit. Gritty, if you let him tell it, was a
Vietnam war hero. Let the neighborhood tell it. He
was the neighborhood bum, slash, drunk. Everybody
took to calling him the "Drunken Master." Today, for
some reason, his words stuck out in his head. No
one could be trusted until he knew for a fact who
sold him out.

Brian and Devon gave each other a pound. Brian
walked him to his truck.

"Tomorrow night, nigga," Brian said.

"Tomorrow night, 6:00, the mall," Devon answered.

Brian watched him pull off. He walked back to
the bench. He sat down, leaned back, and closed his
eyes. Moments later, heaven spoke to him.

"Can I have a cigarette?"

Brian's eyes popped open. "You just can't be creeping up on me like that, Ma."

"I'm not your ma," heaven responded, "and I do have a name. Or did you forget it."

"No, Arlene. How could I ever forget your name?"

Hottie put her hand on her hip. "What's that supposed to mean?"

"C'mon, woman. Stop trying to read into everything I say," Brian said before he turned his attention to her son. "Hey, little man."

"He's got a name or did—"

"Hey, Sherodd," Brian said cutting her off. "How you doing, little man?"

"Fine."

"How old are you now?"

He looked at his mother.

"Tell him."

He looked back at Brian. "I'm five, five years old."

Arlene dug into his jacket pocket and took out the pack of Newports. "Hey, woman. You can't be digging in my pocket like that. You may pull something out you ain't got no business seeing."

"Like what? Your bus pass?"

"No, like a condom or—"

She punched him in the arm. "Watch your mouth, boy. You see him here."

"You hit hard like a dude."

"Give me a light before I hit you like a dude again."

Brian dug into his pocket and held out the lighter. She cocked her head at him. He got the hint. He flicked the lighter and held the flame up for her.

She took a puff off her cigarette before she spoke. "So it's been a year since you graduated from August Martin. What have you done with yourself so far?"

"I've done a lot. You wouldn't know though, because you only come down to the city during the summer vacation to visit your pops."

"Well, if I didn't come down here every summer to spend time with my father, we wouldn't have met because we both know you were never coming up to Albany."

"You're right about that. I would probably get fifty years messing with the crackers and their courts."

"If you doing the right thing, you wouldn't have to worry about the crackers and their courts."

"Say that again."

"What?"

"Cracker."

"What for?"

"That's the closest I've ever heard you come to cursing."

"Boy, you stupid. You still didn't answer my question."

"Well, I've been working off and on. I finally got a steady job at New York Hospital."

"Wow, I don't know what to say?"

"What's that supposed to mean?"

"Stop trying to read into everything I say."

"You got jokes."

She smiled.

How the fuck could a dude share the same bed with her, get her pregnant, and then leave her? He's got to be the stupidest nigga alive, the stupidest nigga ever. They probably made up the label "Stupid Nigga" just for his stupid ass. What attracted him to her so much was that he could be himself around her. There was no image to protect, no prospect of ever sleeping with her, so what did he have to lose?

She took two more pulls off her cigarette before putting it out. "Well, hottie, it's time for me to go."

Brian cocked his head at her, trying to imitate her. "I do have a name. Or did you forget it?"

She grabbed her son's hand. "Bye, Brian. And don't be staring at my butt when I walk off."

"Woman, please, I got your butt in my memory bank. Anytime I want to look at it, I just close my eyes and, bam! there it is."

"Bye, Brian."

"Do you mean it this time?"

She turned and walked off. Sherodd turned back around and waved at him.

Arlene turned around and smiled when she caught Brian staring at her ass.

Brian put on the most innocent face he could muster. "What?" She rolled her eyes and kept walking.

Brian hopped into his truck and took a long swallow of his Heineken before pulling off.

• • •

When Jason woke up, he didn't know where he was. He was quickly reminded when he moved his arm and felt the handcuff.

He looked toward the door and saw a uniformed officer. *Shit,* he thought.

"Yo, officer," Jason called out.

The officer walked into the room. "What's up?"

"I was hoping you could tell me. I was the victim here. Why am I the one cuffed to the bed?"

"The homicide detectives will be here shortly to answer your questions."

"Homicide detectives?"

"Just sit tight."

"This is some bullshit," Jason said.

Last night was a blur. All he could remember, other than being in extreme pain, was officers asking him his name. He gave them the first name that came to mind, James Smith. Then they asked him what happened. "Dudes robbed me" was all he said. When he got to the hospital, he remembered the doctors hooking him up to a machine and shooting some kind of dye in him to see where the bullets had lodged themselves. Then he passed out.

Now, he looked around the room. *There's nothing to worry about,* he told himself. When he looked at his hands, he realized that he spoke too soon. He saw traces of black ink on his fingers. Jason wasn't a religious person, but today was as good as any to call on God, because no man could help him now.

A half hour later, two detectives walked into the room. The white detective with the coal black hair stepped forward, pulling out a pen and pad. "My name's Detective Turner. You want to tell us what happened?"

Jason stared at the ceiling. "I got robbed, and they shot me."

"Who shot you?"

"I don't know."

The detective who stood in the background just stared at him like he wanted to just pull his gun out and pistol whip him. Jason looked at him and nodded. The detective seethed at the gesture.

Detective Turner continued. "So tell us what happened from the beginning."

Jason sighed. "I was on my way to a party, and these guys started walking toward me. I didn't think anything of it 'til one of them pulled out a gun and told me to take off my jewelry. I complied with the motherfuckers, but they still shot me. Bitch ass niggas."

"Can you describe any of them?"

"Nah, it all happened too fast." Jason was getting tired of the question-and-answer session. He lifted his hand up. "Why am I handcuffed to this bed? Y'all acting like I was the one who robbed them motherfuckers."

Both detectives looked at each other.

"What the fuck is going on here?" Jason demanded. "You can't arrest me for anything."

"Well, for one," detective Turner said, "you gave us a false name"— he looked at his pad—"Mr. Jason Simmons."

Jason's heart pounded harder than a racehorse crossing the finish line.

Detective Turner smiled when he saw the blood drain from his face. "Prints don't lie." He flipped the pages on his pad.

"You know what else your prints told us?" He paused as if giving Jason a chance to answer the question. "They told us that you have a warrant in Manhattan. You were arrested for an armed robbery, posted five-hundred dollar bail, and never showed up for your court date."

Jason knew where he was going with all this.

Turner adjusted his tie. "But that's nothing. You're going to love this. We have eye witnesses from last night's shootout."

"Shootout?" Jason said.

"Oh yeah," Turner responded. "They positively identified you as one of three assailants opening fire on a car. A car registered to a Tyrone Carter, a.k.a. Tequan."

"Get the fuck out of here," Jason said.

"Oh there's more. Tequan, the man who you were shooting at last night, was gunned down in cold blood this morning. That makes three murders on that same block in two weeks."

Jason was silent.

"That makes you an accessory to murder. Three murders to be exact."

"Whoa, hold up," Jason said panicking. "I didn't kill three people; I didn't kill anyone."

"True, you didn't murder him, but you know who did. You also know who murdered the other two. So as long as I can place you at the scene, shooting at him last night, which I can because I have two witnesses that can, that's all I need. Even if you wanted to cop out, you're getting life on the back. You do know what that means, don't you?"

Jason closed his eyes.

"That means that every time you go before the parole board, they can hit you with twenty-four months for the rest of your life."

For a minute, no one spoke. Detective Turner closed his pad and put it in his pocket. "Tell us who committed the murders, and we'll work something out."

"The only thing we can work on is you getting me a lawyer," Jason responded.

Detective Turner turned to the other detective. "Read the asshole his rights."

The stone-faced detective finally smiled.

• • •

When Brian walked into the mall, he was surprised to see Bret at the food courts on time. The
mall was crowded as usual, so he felt somewhat se-
cure. When Bret saw him, he waved him over.

Brian scanned the court before walking toward
Bret and taking a seat.

"What up?" Bret asked.

"Same shit, different day," Brian responded.
"Where this nigga at?"

"It's 6:00 now. Give him a couple minutes. Knowing him he probably—"

Brian's attention was stolen by a caramel-complexioned brick house walking their way. Her
Cleopatra hairstyle and cat-shaped eyes were awak-
ening the Mr. Hyde inside. Both of them were shocked
when she sat down at their table. When it became
obvious to her that they were speechless, she spoke.

"Where's the dread?"

Brian blinked in confusion. "The dread?"

"Yeah, the dread."

Brian smiled. "So you're Paula?"

Bret stared at them both confused.

She nodded.

Brian shook his head. "I'm glad I didn't meet
you at the movies that night, 'cause I sure would
have went to that hotel, no questions asked."

"What hotel?" Bret asked.

Paula cut in. "Where is he?"

"He's not here. I didn't see a reason for him to
come."

She looked around the mall, letting him know that she didn't believe him.

"Where's Manny?" Bret asked. "I know he didn't send you."

As if hearing his name, he slid out of the crowd who just gotten off the escalator. He made his way over to them, scanning the area. Paula stood up and held the chair out for him to sit down before she took the seat next to him.

"I got to get me one of those," Bret said, winking at Paula. She rolled her eyes. Bret licked his lips.

"So what's the deal?" Brian said to Manny.

Manny didn't speak right away. He just stared at him for a couple seconds 'til he felt Brian becoming uneasy. "A lot is up, motherfucker."

Brian cocked his head.

Manny smiled. "There's going to be a new king of the hill. The dread made sure of that."

Brian stared at him. "So you're the new king of the hill?"

"Nah, youngin'," Manny said folding his hands. "Why be king of the hill when I can be god of the kings?"

Paula smiled at his wit. Brian wanted to smack her.

"You told me Tequan was in critical condition," Bret said.

"He was, but he didn't make it."

Brian cut in. "So what's up with us?"

Manny sat on the edge of his seat. "Youngin', you talk like you got some balls. You probably don't even have any hair on them yet." Paula busted out laughing.

Brian's face turned red, and he balled his fist up.

"Easy, youngin'," Manny said. He dug into his jacket pocket and pulled out a DVD disc. "Y'all take a look at this and then get back at me."

Bret and Brian looked at the disc as Manny slid it toward them.

"And, youngin'," Manny said, "the next time we meet, you better show me the respect I deserve. I'm god, nigga. I created the game. Learn your history."

Manny and Paula got up and walked off.

Brian looked at Bret. "What the fuck is this?"

"We about to find out," Bret said picking it off the table and heading toward his truck.

• • •

When they got into Bret's truck, he popped the DVD into the truck's DVD player. He adjusted the screen so they could both watch. The scene was as plain as day. The camera zoomed in on Jason's face as he got out of the stolen Acura and headed toward Tequan's car. The camera then zoomed in on Brian and Devon's faces as they got out and followed him. The unknown camera person filmed them shooting at Tequan's car, then them taking Jason's gun and extra clips before fleeing the scene. It didn't take a rocket scientist to know where Manny was going with this.

The only words Bret could say was "Oh, shit."

Brian got an instant headache.

• • •

Bret kept calling Manny, but he only got his answering machine. He hung up and started to call back.

"Don't even waste your time," Brian said. "The motherfucker wants us to stew in our juices for a while."

Bret folded up his phone and put it away. "So what are we going to do?"

"We?" Brian said. "You don't have anything to worry about."

Bret grabbed the pack of Newports off his dashboard and lit one up. "They can't place me at the scene, but that doesn't mean he won't try and use what he has on you to blackmail me."

Brian grabbed the pack of Newports from Bret and lit one up. He rolled the window down and blew the smoke outside. He was silent the whole time he smoked his cigarette. Bret was silent as well. He figured Brian was thinking of a way to get out of this mess. Or maybe he was thinking how long he would allow himself to be blackmailed until he says enough is enough.

His silence was beginning to spook Bret out. So Bret decided to talk about something else.

"So what do you think about Long Island?"

Brian lit another cigarette. "I don't know."

"You don't know as in you can't do it, or you don't know as in you don't know if you want to do it?"

Brian exhaled a cloud of smoke. "Both."

Bret laid his head back on the headrest.

"Listen, man," Brian said, "Jason is lying up in some hospital. I don't know what his condition is; one of my boys might be a rat, and I have no idea which one. Now this nigga Manny got us on fucking videotape shooting at Tequan's car. Shit is hot, Bret. And I'm going to keep it real with you. I know them LI cats ain't just going to let me walk up in there and walk off with half a million dollars and fifty kilos of coke."

"That's the deal, Bee."

"Fuck the deal. You are either the stupidest motherfucker alive, or you're setting me up."

Bret's face became of contortion of anger, surprise, and betrayal. "You ungrateful motherfucker! I can't believe that shit just came out of your mouth. After all the shit I put in your lap."

"Yeah, and after all the times I put my life on the line for you," Brian responded.

"Get the fuck out of my truck!"

Brian opened the door and jumped out. "So when do you want me to come by and pick up that package for LI?"

"Thursday afternoon, same time."

"Okay. I'll talk to the young kid who is supposed to be their inside man. You know, feel him and see what's what."

"Yeah, you do that."

Brian began to walk off. Bret called out to him.

Brian turned back around. "What up?"

"You know that you're a dickhead, right?"

Brian cracked a smile. "I'd rather be a dick than a pussy." Bret rolled up his window and pulled off.

Brian jumped into his truck and called Devon. "Where you at?"

"On the Belt Parkway, heading back to Brooklyn."

"Don't get too close to them."

"Nigga, you ain't talking to no new jack. I got this."

Brian told him what happened at the meeting and about the videotape. Devon was silent all the while. When Brian finished, he waited for Devon to respond.

"You ain't got anything to say?"

"There's nothing to be said. We got to get that tape," Devon said.

"No, shit. How are we gonna do that?"

"When you come up with a plan, let me know." Devon hung up.

Devon never failed to surprise Brian with his uncanny cool composure. If that tape got out, they could all be facing twenty-five to life for each of the three bodies that dropped on that block within a two-week span. And all he said was we got to get that tape.

Brian called Laquana up, praying that she found out where Jason was hospitalized. To his surprise, Teshawna picked up the phone. "Teshawna?"

"What's up, Bee?"

"Where's Laquana?"

"She's upstairs in the bed."

"In the bed?"

"Yeah, she's been calling all around looking for Jay, and she can't locate him. She's thinking the worst 'cause usually when he's in trouble, he calls her. He ain't call or nothing."

"Okay. Can you tell her that I called and that I'm still looking for him as well?"

"Okay."

"And Teshawna, I'm really sorry about—"

"It's no big deal."

"Nah, I just—"

"Really, Bee. It's nothing. There's nothing to talk about."

Brian got the hint. "Well, just tell Laquana that I will call her if I hear anything. And if she hears from him, have her call me."

"Okay."

"Take care."

Teshawna hung up without a response.

Where the fuck are you at, Jay, Brian thought to himself.

• • •

When the detectives dropped Jason off at central booking on Queens Boulevard a couple days ago, he couldn't believe he was going through "the system." When the cell door slammed shut behind him, it was official. The first word that came to his mind to describe the holding pen he was in was *God motherfucking damn.*

There were five men slouched on a bench made for three.

The other men leaned against the wall, while others made themselves comfortable sleeping on the gritty floor. By the looks of their dingy clothes and the smell leaping off of their bodies, they had to be in there for a couple of days. He felt like he was in a toilet that hadn't been flushed in weeks. He stood straight up in the corner, trying not to touch the grime that surrounded him, but who was he fooling? The holding pen, commonly known as the "bull pen," was so grimy that the air was brown.

Jason wondered how long it would take before he looked like the walking dirt that surrounded him. After what seemed like three hours, he couldn't stand anymore. The leg he got shot in was on fire. The correction officers took his crutches from him as soon as he walked in. So he had nothing to lean on. *Fuck it,* he thought. He sat down on the sticky floor.

One of the guys sitting on the bench smiled and turned his head. Jason knew what he was smiling about. He probably wanted to see how long it was going to take for him to stop being "too good" and make himself comfortable. He looked at everyone in the pen and wondered how they looked when they first came in. *How long did it take them to just submit and become part of the grime?*

Just as he was getting comfortable, a correction officer opened the cell door. "All right, let's go."

Everybody got up and lined up to leave the cell. Moments later, they all were herded into another pen and the CO slammed the door behind them. Everyone who was on the bench in the last pen jumped back on the bench and everyone who was sleeping on the floor, laid back on the floor and went back to sleep.

Jason caught Smiley looking at him. "When are we going to see a judge?"

Smiley shrugged his shoulders. "If not today, maybe tomorrow?"

"Tomorrow!"

"We still got two more pens to go into before we see the judge."

"Two more pens?"

"Yeah," Smiley said. "Welcome to bull pen therapy."

• • •

Brian spent the rest of the week at Sonia's house. She was always complaining about him never spending enough time with her, but now she felt suffocated as he sat on the couch across from her and watched her study for her exams. Every now and then, she would look up at him from over her glasses and smile at him. Unbeknown to her, Brian was aging her in his mind. He imagined how she would look ten years from now. *What type of mother would she be? What type of wife would she be? Wife, whoa, that word itself sounded old.* Until that moment, marriage was just a fleeing thought. Today, it occupied his mind.

Sonia looked up again and caught him staring at her. "What?"

Brian seemed confused. "What?"

"You're creeping me out."

"I'm creeping you out?"

"Yeah, you're just sitting there staring at me."

"I can't stare at you?"

"No, you can't. That's rude."

"Rude? You're my wife. I can't stare at you whenever I want?"

Sonia cocked her head. "Excuse me? Umm, when did I become your wife?"

"C'mon, baby stop playing," Brian said, laughing.

Sonia didn't crack a smile.

Brian stopped smiling. "What?"

"Your way of asking me to marry you is getting me pregnant?"

Brian sat back on the couch. "Woman, you bugging out. You know, you wifey, so knock it off."

Sonia took off her glasses. "And when did you make this decision?"

"Okay, all right already," Brian said.

"No, it's not all right. You got some nerve. You just tell me that I am you're wife and that's that?"

The sirens went off in his head. *Time to buckle up, we're about to hit some turbulence,* he said to himself.

"I'm not marrying you."

Brian laughed. "Yeah, okay. Stop playing."

Sonia didn't laugh.

Brian continued to laugh, but out of the corner of his eye, he saw that she was dead serious.

Brian's ego was hurt. So he did what he did best. "Well, to be honest, the only reason why I was going to marry you is because you're having my baby. But now, after that shit you just said, I don't even know if it's mine."

Sonia's eyes got big like saucers.

Brian was livid, he got up and started heading out the door. "Go and marry the nigga that got you pregnant." He slammed the front door, praying that she would come running outside to stop him from leaving. She wasn't like Andrea though.

As he drove off, his cell phone rang. He smiled when he saw it was Sonia.

"What?"

"I swear on my parents and on my baby, if you ever come in arm distance of me, I will cut you from your ear all the way down to your crooked dick."

Click!

Brian, on many occasions, witnessed Sonia's carving technique. And there are a lot of scar-faced bitches walking around because of her. *I'll give her a few days to calm down then I'll have Laquana talk to her,* he said to himself.

Just then, his phone rang. He thought it was Sonia.

"Listen, baby, I'm sorry I didn't—"

"Bee, it's Quana?"

"Oh, hey."

"Jason just called me."

"Is he all right? Where is he?"

Laquana started crying. "He's on Rikers Island."

"What!"

"I have to see him, Bee."

"Not a problem. I'll come by about eight in the morning—"

"No, I have to see him today."

Brian paused for a couple seconds. "Yeah...okay. I'll be there in about fifteen minutes."

"Thank you."

"No problem."

He hung up and called Devon. "Jay is at Rikers Island."

"What did they arrest him for?"

"I don't know. I'm going up there with Laquana now to see what the deal is."

"You're not going in, right?"

"Hell no!"

"Cool."

"Where the fuck you been anyway? I haven't heard from you in a couple days."

"You know that bitch that Manny sent at me?"

"Yeah."

"She's got a twin sister."

"Damn, that's crazy." Brian thought for a moment. "How you know that?"

That day when I followed Manny and the bitch to Brooklyn, he dropped her home first. Before the bitch got out the car, the twin comes walking out the house. The one in the car gets out and goes inside. The other one gets into the car.

"She's talking to Manny for a few moments, and then boom! Just like that, she disappears. A few moments later, Manny is jerking like he's on an electrical fence, then the bitch pops back up wiping her mouth with the back of her hand."

"That lucky motherfucker," Brian said. "I think if anybody knows where Manny stashed the original tape it's her." Brian didn't want to know how he was going to get her to tell him the location of the tape. "Let me know when you get something."

"No doubt."

• • •

When Brian pulled up to Laquana's house, she was outside, sitting on the porch. Teshawna was sitting next to her, trying to console her. Laquana looked like she had aged ten years.

Brian got out the truck and walked to the porch.

153

Laquana was the darkest girl Brian ever saw in his life.

She was jet black with chinky eyes. Now she was pale, and her eyes were almost swollen shut from all the crying she had been doing. Brian didn't know what to say to her.

She stood up with the help of Teshawna and hugged him. When he put his arms around her, her dam of tears broke. Teshawna's eyes welled up with tears.

Brian squeezed her. "We're going to get him out of there, Quana."

She shook her head against his chest and spoke between her sobs. "He said he's really in deep. He doesn't know if he's coming home this time."

"C'mon, Quana. Don't talk like that."

"It's not me, it's him. He said he may have to do some time."

Brian felt her legs give out and struggled to hold her up. "C'mon. Let's go and see him."

They all got into his truck.

On their way to Rikers Island, no one said a word. Brian never saw Laquana this distraught. This wasn't the first time Jason had been arrested. He did time on the island before. *What did she know for her to be on the verge of having a nervous breakdown?*

They finally pulled up to Rikers Island. Brian cut the engine off and looked over at Laquana. She was shaking.

"Quana, I'll wait here for you and Teshawna."

"I'm not going in there without you."

"Quana, it's no big deal."

"I can't go in there and see him like that by myself."

"Teshawna is going in with you."

Laquana turned around and gave her a venomous stare. "Did you know that he was fucking her?"

Brian's mouth dropped open.

"Don't lie to me, Brian. Did you know?"

Brian was too shocked to answer.

Laquana started hitting him. "Don't lie to me. Brian, did you know?"

Brian grabbed her hands. "Quana, calm the fuck down!" Teshawna started crying.

"This is not helping anybody right now, Quana," Brian said. Brian felt the tension leaving her body.

"He's a dog, Brian. A fucking dog. Of all the people in the world, why her?"

Brian didn't know what to say. Everything was happening too fast.

Laquana got out of the truck and slammed the door. She walked over to Brian's side and waited for him to get out. "You're going in with me to confront him."

Teshawna opened her door to get out.

"No, bitch. You stay right here," Laquana hissed.

Teshawna complied without hesitation.

Laquana stared at Brian, waiting for him to get out of the truck. He shook his head and got out. "I don't think this is a good idea." Without a word, Laquana grabbed his hand and headed in.

• • •

While Brian and Laquana sat at the square table waiting for Jason to come down, Brian's heart was pounding like a jackhammer. He had no way of fore-warning Jason about what was about to go down. Laquana's mind was made up. She was done with him. There was nothing Brian could say that would convince her otherwise.

Fifteen minutes later, Jason came from out the back walking with crutches. Laquana covered her mouth and started crying.

Yes, Brian thought. *All that shit she was talking was just a front. All she needed was to see him.* She got up and walked to him. When he bent down to kiss her, she smacked him. It seemed like everyone in the room turned toward the sound.

Jason was stunned. Laquana stunned him one more time on the other side of his face.

As Jason hobbled back, Brian jumped up and grabbed her hand. "Quana, what the fuck are you doing?"

"Get off of me!" She charged toward Jason who was still in shock.

Brian grabbed her by the waist. She clawed at his hands and arms. "Get off of me!" She squirmed in Brian's arms trying to get at Jason.

"What the fuck is wrong with you?" Jason shouted at her.

"You fucking bastard. You want to sleep with my cousin? My fourteen-year-old cousin?"

Jason's face turned beet red. "What the fuck are you talking about?" Jason asked as innocently as he could.

When Laquana realized she couldn't get out of Brian's grip, she took off her shoe and threw it at Jason and then spit at him.

The COs laughed and let the drama go on for a couple more minutes before they decided to haul Jason away.

When the COs got in between them, Jason got a little heart. "I'm gonna fuck you up when I get out of here. Watch what I do to you!"

Brian picked her off the floor and carried her out the visiting room. "What the fuck is wrong with you?"

Laquana sat on the plastic chair heaving.

"I didn't come all the way up here for this bullshit," Brian said. "This is bullshit."

Laquana rolled her eyes.

Brian grabbed her by the chin. "Don't roll your fucking eyes at me."

Laquana pulled away from him. "Get off of me."

"You know what?" Brian said. "I'm out of here." He walked off, heading back to his truck. Laquana followed him.

When they got back to the truck, Teshawna didn't have to ask what happened. It was written all over their faces.

When Brian pulled up in front of Laquana's house, Laquana opened her mouth to speak.

"Get the fuck out," Brian said.

"I can't believe you're mad at me." Laquana said.

"You didn't even give him a chance."

"A chance?"

"Yeah," Brian said, "a chance. There's two sides to every story."

"What is there to tell? He cheated on me. He got my cousin pregnant. End of story."

Brian looked at Teshawna. "You act like she wasn't wit it. She's just as guilty as him. I don't see you smacking her around and spitting in her face."

"She's only fourteen."

"Give me a break," Brian spat out. "She wasn't acting like a fourteen year-old when she was spreading her legs. She knew what she was doing. She knew who she was fucking, and she didn't give a fuck about you, cousin or no cousin."

Laquana put her head down and opened the truck door. Teshawna got out with her.

"Don't believe the nigga," Teshawna whispered in her ear. Laquana pushed her away.

Brian pulled off, leaving Laquana and Teshawna in the street arguing. He had an appointment in LI.

Chapter 28

When Brian pulled up to the block, he felt all eyes on him.

The LI cats and kittens were nodding to Nas's "Street's Disciple" that was pumping out of his stereo. He parked down the block and walked back to the boulevard.

Equality was the first one he locked eyes with. Equality nodded and smiled. Brian nodded back.

Knowledge was the first one to speak to him. "Peace, god. What the deal?" He slapped Brian five and gave him a hug.

"Same shit, different smell."

Knowledge smiled. "Yeah, no doubt. Let me go get Powerful; he's in the bar."

"I'll be over here"—Brian said pointing to the mob of dudes shooting dice—"watching the game."

Brian got caught up in the game. There was a young slim kid raking in all the loot. "Four, five, six, nigga. Gimme mine," he shouted.

Equality threw a stack of bills at him. "Take that horseshoe out your ass."

"I'm Skillz, nigga. Ain't nothing lucky about me."

Brian could tell Equality was getting upset by the way he would flex his chest every time Skillz would snatch the money off the floor.

"Yo, Born," Skillz called out to Brian, holding the dice out to him. "You want to get in?"

Brian shook his head. "With the way you rolling, I might as well save you the trouble and just give you all my money right now."

Skillz smiled. "True dat."

Brian liked Skillz. He had an aura about him that reminded him of how he was back in his innocent days. Skillz had to be no more than sixteen and had the physique of a basketball player.

The streets hadn't sunk their claws into him fully. He didn't have the beady eyes and gorilla walk yet.

Then again, Brian thought. *The streets didn't make us thugs overnight. There's a grooming process. For most of us, it starts with being intrigued with the rawness of the streets. All the things our parents told us to stay away from— alcohol, cigarettes, drugs, guns, skank women, and hoodlums— were all in front of us, and they appeared to be harmless. We smoked cigarettes because it made us look cool, we drank because it made us look grown, and we dabbled with drugs because it was a quick way to make a buck. we carried guns because of the sense of power it gave us, we messed with skank women because they were the only ones who let us stick our tiny dicks in them, and we emulated the hoodlums because everyone in the neighborhood feared them, including our parents. In the beginning, the streets only showed us love. But when we committed our lives to it, we had seen the other side—the brutal beat downs, the rapes, the stabbings, the shootings, and the murders.*

Brian took a good look at Skillz with his white teeth and wide eyes. Because it would only be a matter of time before he became one of them.

"Skillz! C'mon and roll the fucking dice," Equality said.

Skillz ducked back into the crowd and started trash talking.

Powerful finally stumbled out of the bar with Knowledge. "Yo, Born. What up, god?"

Brian cocked his head. "Why y'all keep calling me Born?"

"The gods wanted to know your name," Powerful answered. "And since everybody got a righteous name, we had to give you one, god."

"Why Born?"

Powerful shrugged his shoulders. "Your name starts with a *B,* so we said fuck it, Born it is."

Brian didn't even try to understand. He walked to his truck with Powerful. When he handed Powerful the knapsack of drugs, Powerful handed it off to one of his little men.

The night air was doing Powerful some good, he was starting to sober up. "So what up, Bee? You come up with a plan yet."

"Nah, not yet."

"What happened to all that getting the juices to flow and rubbing two ideas together bullshit you was talking last week?"

"I'm still rubbing then together."

Powerful laughed.

Brian didn't. "I need to talk to your inside, man, for myself to see exactly how they got everything set up in that house."

Powerful eyed him for a moment. "Yeah, we can do that."

They headed back up to the boulevard. Powerful tapped Knowledge and whispered in his ear. A couple seconds later, Equality and Skillz headed into the strip club.

They got to be kidding, Brian thought to himself.

When Brian and Powerful entered the club, Brian saw Knowledge and Equality sitting at their normal table in the back.

When they approached the table, Powerful introduced Brian to Skillz.

Brian shared with Skillz what Knowledge told him about the spot. Skillz nodded all the while. When Brian finished, he said, "So is there anything else I should know?"

"That's it, pretty much."

Brian could see Equality's eyes on the strippers, but his ears were on their conversation.

Brian had one more question for him. "If y'all can't leave the spot once you go in, what do y'all do for food?"

"It depends. Sometimes we bring in our own shit or we order out."

Brian nodded. For the next hour, he engaged the kid in small talk, while they watched in amazement at how the girls twisted themselves in unbelievable positions.

One of Powerful's little soldiers ran up inside the club and told him that Jamaica was out front. Everybody at the table, except Brian, got up and headed outside. Brian decided to go see what was happening.

When he stepped out the club, Powerful, Knowledge, Equality, Skillz, and a couple other guys had Jamaica surrounded.

"Didn't we tell you not to be up here, Jamaica?" Equality asked.

"Listen, I don't want no trouble. I'm just selling weed, nothing else."

"I don't give a fuck what you're selling," Equality shot back at him. "You can't do it around here."

"It's just weed, I'm not—"

Powerful's fist knocked Jamaica's words back down his throat.

Jamaica covered up as the pack of wolves punched and kicked him to the ground. Powerful ripped the dread's pockets, taking his money and bags of weed.

Jamaica summoned the strength to crawl then run to his car that was parked across the street. Brian now saw girls chasing after him as well punching him in the back of his head and clawing at his neck for his gold chains.

Powerful, Knowledge, and Equality watched from across the street as the mob of shorties pinned Jamaica against his car and continued beating him down. It was a miracle that he managed to get his car door open and slide in. One of the shorties ran across the street with a mini sledgehammer and hit Jamaica's windshield. The kid swung it again, and the windshield started to cave in.

The dread started his car and skidded off.

Powerful was in tears and holding his stomach. "Oh, shit! You saw that, god?" he asked Brian. "That was some funny shit." Brian just smiled.

Brian saw red lights flashing in his peripheral. Everybody scattered like roaches, but there was no place to run. Two cop cars converged on the corner from opposite directions, and two unmarked cars raced up the middle of the block.

Powerful tapped Brian. "You ain't got anything on you, right?"

"Nah, I'm clean."

"We ain't got nothing to worry about then."

One of the unmarked cars pulled up right in front of them. From all the stories Brian heard of Robocop, he knew without a doubt that he was the one who jumped out of the car and was charging at him like a rhino.

"Put your hands in the air, now!"

Just as Brian started to comply, Robocop leaped off the ground and hurled his body into him like a human spear. His shoulder connected with Brian's sternum, folding him in half as they hit the concrete.

Robocop flipped him on his stomach and lodged his knee in the middle of his back. "Fucking punk! When I say put your hands in the air, I mean put your fucking hands in the air." He grabbed a handful of Brian's hair and pinned the side of his face to the pavement.

The pebbles and dirt dug into his cheek, but he didn't dare complain.

Robocop cuffed him and dug into Brian's pockets. He picked him up by the hair and belt loops and slammed him up against the wall.

"What the fuck are you doing in Long Island?" Robo asked Brian.

"He's visiting friends!" Powerful barked.

"Shut your fucking mouth, Michael, before I shove those gold teeth down your throat."

"You ain't doing a motherfucking thing to me, pig."

Brian was on the verge of tears and shaking like a pair of naked dice, and here was Powerful screaming at this cop like he was a bitch.

Brian drew some courage from Powerful's fear-lessness and spoke up, "Yeah, I'm visiting some friends."

Robocop looked around. "Friends?"

"Yeah, those girls sitting over there." Brian gestured with his head.

Robocop called out to them. "Y'all know him?"

One of the girls spoke up. "Yeah, that's Crystal's man."

Brian had no idea who Crystal, was but he ran with it. "Yeah, Crystal's my girlfriend."

Robocop grabbed him by the back of the neck. "So where you stashed the drugs at, huh?"

"There ain't no drugs here! Why you keep fucking with us, pig?" Powerful spat on the ground.

Like a scene straight out of the *Matrix,* Robocop with lightening speed slid up on Powerful and wrapped his massive hands around his neck, choking the life out of him. The two detectives cuffed Powerful and then pried Robocop's hands from around his neck.

Powerful was on one knee, grasping for air. "You fucking coward! All you do is hide behind that badge. You's a bitch."

Robocop grinned; he turned back to Brian. "What the fuck you looking at?" he yelled in Brian's ear as he palmed the back of his head and forced him to face the wall.

For the next few moments, uniformed cops searched the area for any kind of drug paraphernalia. All the while, Brian could hear the little kids calling the police *pigs, crackers,* and *blue-eyed devils.* Brian was trying his best not to laugh.

Robocop nudged the back of his head with his forearm. "What the fuck you smiling at?"

"Nothing."

"Nothing? You smile for no reason?"

Brian didn't respond. He could see his hands wrapped around his neck, choking the life out of him if he got him mad enough. "I just want to go home, sir?"

"Home?" Robocop said astonished. "You're under arrest, you're going to jail."

It was Brian's turn to be astonished. "What am I going to jail for? I didn't do anything."

"You didn't do anything? Hey fellas, he said he didn't do anything." The officers started laughing.

"You woke up this morning, didn't you? You put on these expensive clothes and this nice gold chain." He grabbed Brian's chain and yanked it like he was trying to pop it off his neck. "The mistake you made though was when you decided to come to my town and as you say 'visit some friends.' That is enough reason for me to arrest your punk ass."

The cops turned them all around and told them to stand still against the wall. A cop car cruised by them. Brian was shocked when he saw the dread in the back of the car, holding his head and pointing out Equality and Powerful.

Robocop smiled and told the detectives to put both of them in the back of the car.

Chapter 29

Brian sat on the living room couch, waiting for Bret to come downstairs.

Earlier when Trish answered the door, she didn't look at him or say a word. She just walked back to her room and slammed the door. In their brief encounter, Brian could tell from her stiff posture that she no longer felt comfortable around him. She'd seen a part of him that no one outside of the game ever saw. He thought back to the day when he returned to high school after doing eight months on Rikers Island. Each time, he explained to one of his teachers where he'd been and why they all had the same shocked look glued to their faces.

Brian's attention went to the dining room where they had staged their fight scene. Scuff marks from the chairs, and Bret's head sketched the wall. He wondered what Bret had told his mother. Knowing Bret, he probably didn't tell her how it happened. He probably just told her that he would have it fixed and further pacified her by leaving a couple hundred dollars on her dresser. She knew what her son was into, but she didn't say anything. She was the type of mother who would play dumb until she got a call from Bret telling her that he'd got arrested. Then she would fuss on and on about suspecting that he was into something but didn't know what. Then she would ask him why he couldn't just find a job instead of selling drugs.

Brian, for the life of him, could never understand why parents did that. *If I ever suspect my son or daughter of ever doing anything illegal,* Brian thought, *I will bring it to them straight up.*

When Bret came downstairs, he handed him the phone without a word.

Brian spoke into it. "Yeah."

"What up, youngin'?"

Brian could picture the cheesy grin on Manny's face.

"Same shit, different smell."

"Your man told me y'all were trying to get in touch with me for the past week. I apologize for not getting back at you sooner."

Brian could hear the sarcasm seeping out of his words.

"How much do you want for the tape?" Brian asked, getting right down to business.

"It's not for sale."

Brian remained silent. He wasn't going to play the back-and-forth game with him.

When Manny realized he couldn't twist Brian's nuts in knots, like he did with Bret, he continued. "I like you, youngin', you got heart. I'll give you that."

Manny let his words sink in before he continued. "To be honest with you, I think Bret doesn't know what he has at his disposal."

"Is that right?" Brian said sarcastically.

"You got the mental, the muscle, and the majesty to be—"

"King of the hill?" Brian said, finishing his sentence.

"Nah," Manny answered. "The king of kings."

"Actually, I wanted to be the god of kings."

"That spot's already taken, youngin'."

"For how long?"

"For as long as I have this videotape."

"So when do we meet?"

"I'll let you know, youngin'"

Manny hung up, leaving Brian on pins and needles until the next time they spoke.

"So what did he say?" Bret asked.

"He ain't say shit. I asked him how much he wanted for the tape, and he said it wasn't for sale."

"What does he want then?"

"He said he'll call me back."

"This nigga's got to be taken care of," Bret said, shuffling back and forth the length of the living room.

Brian dug in his coat pocket and pulled out the wad of money he collected from last night's run in

Long Island. Bret looked at the money and forgot all about Manny.

"Equality and Powerful got arrested last night," Brian said throwing the money on the coffee table.

"How? What happened?"

"They beat some Jamaican kid up, because he was selling some weed on their corner. The cops must have been watching the corner, because as soon as the dread pulled off, it seemed like the whole precinct raided the corner."

"You serious?"

"Yeah. And I got to meet Robocop face to fist."

Bret couldn't help laughing. "Is he as bad as they say he is?"

"Worse."

Brian related the story blow by blow. Then told him how Knowledge stepped up and took over the operations.

"He told me that he was going to bail them out as soon as they saw the judge and got a bail," Brian said.

Hearing the word *bail* made Bret think of Jason. "So what's up with Jay?"

"I'm waiting on the call." A thought ran through his head.

"When did Manny call you?"

"Right after you got here."

"Did you tell him I was here?"

Bret shook his head. "Nah." He cocked his head, knowing what Brian was thinking. "After I told him what I thought of the tape, he told me to put you on the phone. Maybe he just assumed you were here."

"He doesn't strike me as the assuming type."

Brian pulled out his cell phone and called Devon. Devon answered on the third ring. "What's up?"

"Where you at?"

"I'm sitting a block away from the twins' house."

"How long you been there?"

"Since I followed them here from Green Acres."

"That was a week ago, Dev."

"It feels like a year."

"Don't you think you may start to look kind of suspicious sitting out there?"

"Nah, I switch cars every night. I'm getting good at hot wiring. I'm almost as good as—"

"Yeah, I know," Brian said. "Jay hasn't called me yet. If I don't hear from him by tomorrow, I'm going to the island to see him."

"Cool."

"That's not the reason why I called you. I'm supposed to start that job at the hospital tomorrow morning. So I need you to do something."

"What's that?"

"I need you to follow somebody."

"Who?"

Devon smiled when Brian told him who and why.

Chapter 30

Brian was surprised to see Marilyn waiting for him at the door of the janitor's locker room. He faked an alarmed look. "I swear, whatever it is, I didn't do it. I didn't even punch in yet."

Marilyn looked at him questioningly. She didn't get the joke.

"No, Brian. You didn't do anything wrong. I just wanted to introduce you to Kenny. He's going to do your orientation."

Kenny must have heard his name because he came switching out the locker room. "Hey, Ms. Marilyn."

"How you doing, Kenny?"

Kenny stared at Brian when he answered her question. "I'm feeling much better."

Oh, hell no! Brian shouted to himself. *I know this bitch ain't trying to pair me up with this fag.*

"Kenny, this is Brian. And, Brian, this is Kenny."

Kenny stuck his hand out. "Pleasure's all mine."

Brian shook his hand with an intimidating grip. He pulled his hand back when he saw the fag was actually enjoying the pain. Brian kept swallowing to keep from tasting the bile that was gathering in his throat.

Marilyn could see the awkwardness in Brian's face. "Kenny will show you what you have to do. Once you get it down packed, you'll be on your own."

The only thing that kept Brian from cursing her out and telling Kenny to suck his dick was, number one, Kenny may actually try to suck his dick, and number two, he would never hear the end of it from his mother. So he held his tongue and gave Marilyn a stare that could melt the sun, then walked into the locker room.

• • •

A few moments later, Kenny walked in.

"I know you don't like me, but don't worry, you'll like me once you get to know me."

Is it me, Brian thought, *or is it that every time this dude says something it has some type of sexual undertone?* He decided to set the record straight before shit got out of hand.

"Listen, here. I ain't one of those dudes who you be flirting with."

"Boy, please. I'm not even thinking about you. I got plenty of men who want me," Kenny said, running his hands down his chest and around his butt.

"Yeah, well save that homo shit for them."

"Excuse you?"

Brian dropped his duffle bag and moved toward him with clenched fists. His mind was made up. If this chump said one more smart remark, he was going to break his jaw.

"I said, save that homo shit for them. You got a problem with that?"

"All right, all right! You ain't got to get all up in a brother's space," Kenny said, dropping his voice a couple octaves.

For the next few hours, Kenny worked and Brian watched. To his surprise, everyone they came in contact with loved Kenny.

Every time he finished talking with them, he would tell Brian the "real deal" about the person. Brian was impressed with the amount of personal information Kenny knew, and the amount of orderlies and doctors he did "favors" for. By the end of the day, Brian had the "real deal" on everyone, including Ms. Freaky, Marilyn Thomas.

For the next few days, Brian looked forward to going to work just to hear all the gossip Kenny had to share. On his second day there, unbeknown to Kenny, he actually gave Brian the idea on how he was going to rob the drug spot in LI.

Kenny had asked him if he got high. When Brian asked him why, he told him that he could get him all the pills and drugs he wanted. He explained to Brian how he got all his drugs and what not from a doctor who he was exchanging favors with. When Brian asked him if he could get him some liquid morphine,

Kenny nodded and told him he would have it for him when they punched out.

To his surprise, Kenny handed him four bottles of liquid morphine in the locker room. When Brian went in his pocket to pay him, Kenny grabbed his hand and told him not to worry about it.

Brian eyed him suspiciously.

Kenny picked up on it right away. "Ain't nobody want you," he said in a mocking tone. "You are not all that, okay? What you need to do is get back in the good graces of the woman who's having your baby."

Brian surprised himself by telling Kenny all about the drama he had with Sonia on his first day at the job. Kenny had given him some sound advice, some real good advice, but his pride wouldn't allow him to cave in. He missed Sonia terribly, but he refused to be the one to bend.

"Fuck you, Kenny."

Kenny smiled.

Brian's face turned red.

"What?" Kenny said. "You said it."

Brian stared at him.

Kenny stared back. "What?"

"Nothing," Brian said. "I just can't see a doctor who's married with kids fucking with you."

"Negro, please," Kenny said, rolling his eyes, "I've lost track of all the married men I've done, sucked, and fucked."

"Why would they put their careers and marriages on the line for you?"

Kenny batted his eyes. "They can't resist me 'cause I'm their forbidden fruit."

"Forbidden fruit?"

"I let men do to me what their wives would never allow." Brian seemed confused.

Kenny sighed. "For example, Dr. Harris. You know who he is right?"

"Yeah, late forties, chubby, with the bald spot."

"Well," Kenny said, "when he sticks his wee wee halfway into his wife's mouth, she gags." Kenny started laughing. "One time, she threw up on his dick."

Brian started laughing.

Kenny continued. "All over his shit, I ain't lying. Now with me," Kenny said, smacking his lips, "he can grab the back of my head and ram his wee wee all the way down my throat. I done mastered my gag reflex."

Brian couldn't believe he was having this conversation.

Kenny continued, oblivious to the fact that Brian stopped laughing. "And when he cums, it's like Maxwell House coffee, good to the last drop."

"All right, all right already, enough. I get it now."

Kenny put his hand on his hip. "I'm sorry. I just wanted to draw you a picture. Was I a little too graphic?"

Brian slammed his locker shut and walked out. When he got to his truck, he smiled. He knew Kenny didn't mean any harm. He actually felt sorry for him. He tried to imagine all the molestations and rapes little Kenny must have endured before convincing himself that he may as well profit from his pain.

Brian drove off and headed toward Rikers Island. Jason hadn't called him or Laquana since the episode in the visiting room.

When Brian waited in the visiting room for Jason to come down, he replayed the conversation he had with Knowledge over the phone. Knowledge told him that he bailed Equality and Powerful out on Monday. Then, the very next day, Robocop came around and arrested them for tampering with a witness. Robocop supposedly got the dread to say that as soon as Equality and Powerful got out, they went to his house and threatened to kill him if he came to court.

That sounded like something they would do, but Brian didn't want to share that with Knowledge. He did tell him that he had a way to pull off the job, but the only catch was that it had to be done this weekend. Knowledge didn't know what to say, it wasn't his call.

Brian knew that he would have a better chance at getting away with it if Equality and Powerful were still in the county jail. He finally convinced him that if they didn't do it this weekend, it wouldn't get done; and when Equality and Powerful found out that he made it happen, they would respect his leadership skills to the fullest.

So it was on. Saturday night, according to Skillz, was the time when they were sitting on the most money and drugs.

When Jason walked in, Brian stopped breathing. He stood up to greet his pale and skinny friend.

"Damn, nigga. You lost a lot of weight. They ain't feeding you up in here or something?"

"I can't eat this shit," Jason grumbled. "I wouldn't even feed this shit to my dog."

Brian tried to lift his spirits. "Well, you got to eat it. I put some money in your account so you can go to commissary and buy whatever you want."

"They don't sell freedom in commissary, Bee."

Brian put his head down. "So what they talking about?"

"Fucking cops are trying to charge me the three murders."

"What!" Brian regained his composure, then whispered, "How the fuck they gonna pin three murders on you? They ain't got no evidence, no witnesses, no nothing." Brian didn't tell him about the videotape Manny had, no sense in stressing him out about that.

"Well, in this day and time, they don't need any of that to get a conviction," Jason said. "All the DA got to do is paint the picture to the jury that it was some kind of drug beef, and I'm the reason why their babies are getting hit with stray bullets, and that's it."

"No, that's not it. They got to find you guilty beyond a shadow of a doubt."

Brian just may as well have been talking to a brick wall, because Jason wasn't listening.

"We're gonna get you a good lawyer."

"A good lawyer for three bodies, do you know how much that's going to cost?"

"Don't worry about the cost."

Jason changed the subject. "How's Quana?"

"I talked to her a couple days ago. She's okay."

"She's my heart, Bee."

"Yeah, I know."

"I can't afford to lose her," Jason said, becoming teary eyed.

"She just needs some time to get over what happened, Jay."

"I need to be out there with her. I don't want no nigga taking advantage of her while she's at her weakest point."

"I got my eyes on her, Jay. Stop stressing her. She ain't gonna do nothing that stupid."

Jason stared off in space again.

Brian spent the next thirty-five minutes trying to convince him that he was going to beat everything in trial. And that Laquana was going to be there when he got home.

After the visit, Brian went to the schoolyard and sat on the bench. Two minutes later, he was fast asleep.

• • •

Brian nearly jumped off the bench when Arlene poked him in the ribs. He looked around disoriented before he focused on her.

"What are you doing out here sleep?"

"I wasn't sleeping."

She pointed to his jacket. "So why you drooling?

Brian looked down at the stain on his jacket. "That's not drool."

"So what is it then?"

"Why you ask so many questions?"

"Why you don't give straight answers?"

Brian reached into his pocket and realized he left his cigarettes in his truck. "Give me a cigarette."

"I know your mama raised you better than that."

"Can I have a cigarette, please, Ms. Arlene?"

"Damn, why you got to say my name like I'm all old and whatnot?"

Brian reached out to grab her. "Woman, just give me a cigarette before you make me hurt you."

She swatted his hand away. "Calm down." She reached into her pocket and pulled out a pack of Salem Lights. "Here."

Brian looked at her like she just handed him a box of rat poison. "Unbelievable." He got up and brushed past her toward his truck.

"What's your problem?" she called after him.

He ignored her and grabbed the pack of Newports off his dashboard.

"I should've left your grouchy ass sleep," she said as she walked off.

After Brian took two long pulls on his cigarette, he ran after her. "Hey, you know I didn't mean no harm. I'm grouchy when I first wake up, that's all."

She kept walking as if she didn't hear him.

"I'm sorry. Please slow down so we can talk."

"We don't have anything to talk about."

"I have a lot to talk to you about."

She stopped and faced him.

Brian was stunned when he saw her watery eyes. He instantly wanted to smash his head against the wall a thousand times. He barely knew her, but at that moment, he made a vow to never hurt her ever again.

"What do you have to talk about?" she asked.

"Can we sit down?" he said, pointing to the benches. She followed him.

When they sat down, Brian grabbed her hand. "I'm about to tell you something and please don't take it the wrong way."

She nodded.

"I'm jealous of you," Brian said.

Arlene pulled her hand back and started to get up. "I don't have time to play no games with you."

"I'm serious," Brian said, grabbing her hand. "Just hear me out." She sat back down, but refused to look at him.

"Listen, when I see you and Sherodd playing on the monkey bars or on the swings, y'all look so happy. Every time I go to see my son, I always get into a fight, whether it's his mother, her sisters, or one of their baby daddies. Now, my girl, who is pregnant, doesn't want to have anything to do with me. My parents are two seconds from disowning me, and people who I thought were my friends may not really be my friends." She made eye contact with him.

"You are the only one who I haven't tainted with my bullshit, and I want to keep it like that."

"Why don't you just get out of the game then?"

Brian cocked his head. "What do you mean?"

"Let's not play stupid. You know what I mean. It may not look like it, but I was caught up in the bullshit that you're talking about." Brian looked at her surprised.

"Sherodd's father was in 'the game,' and he went through all the 'bullshit' you're talking about right now. I'm going to tell you the same thing I told him. In the 'game' that y'all are playing, there are no winners. Some of y'all just take a little longer to lose. Sherodd's father lost. He lost me, he lost his son, and he lost his life."

Brian squeezed her hand. "I'm sorry to hear that."

"Don't be sorry. Don't make the same mistake he did. Get out before you lose."

He locked eyes with her. That moment would forever be etched into his mind with the kiss she softly placed on his lips. A feeling stirred inside him that he never felt. Not only did he not know what it was, but he couldn't even describe it. He pulled away from her; he didn't want to taint the only pure thing in his life. "I got to go."

She stood and wiped her eye and smiled. "Okay. I guess I'll see you around then."

"You definitely will."

When Brian got to his truck, he heard his cell phone ringing. It was Devon.

"What up?"

"You are the motherfucking man, Bee."

"Oh, yeah?"

"Oh, yeah. She lead me right to the snitch."

"Say no more. Where you at?"

"In front of her house."

"I'll be there in twenty minutes."

"Cool."

Chapter 31

When Brian turned on to Bret's block, he saw Devon leaning on the side of a grey cargo van. Brian parked behind him.

"I hope you got some good news for me," Brian said as he got out his truck.

"When you told me stick to Trish, I thought you were out of your mind," Devon said while getting into the van.

Brian got in on the passenger side. "Yeah, well, I didn't want to believe it was you or Jason, so she was the only one outside of the circle who may have a clue.

Brian thought back to the times he caught her standing in front of Bret's room or by the staircase listening in on their conversations. He knew he would be crushed if she was the mole, but he wouldn't be surprised.

"So run it down to me," Brian said.

"First of all, let me just tell you that she ain't got any friends."

Brian shrugged his shoulders. "What does that have to do with anything?"

"You'll see. Anyway, after school, when everybody's scrambling to get home and do what they got to do, Trish's sitting on the curb. At first, I thought she was waiting for Bret or her mom to come pick her up, but then a red Volkswagen Jetta pulled up. The chick looked to be about a young eighteen. Trish springs off the curb, wearing a smile bigger than the state of Texas and hops in. I followed them to Macy's, the Gap, and Dr. Denim. They came out of each store with at least four bags." Devon stared at Brian for a second.

"What?"

Devon shook his head.

"What? What the fuck?"

"Did you fuck her?"

"You're gonna stop in the middle of the story to ask me if I was fucking her?"

Devon stared at him.

Brian hit the dashboard. "Yes, I fucked her."

"Did she like it?"

Brian took a deep breath, and without warning, he popped Devon on the side of the head.

"Whoa!" Devon said, putting his arm up to block the second blow. "I'm just fucking with you."

"Now is not the time."

"All right, fuck it. So the chick drops her home and helps her bring all the bags into the house."

"All the bags were for Trish?"

"Every last one. When Trish walked her to the front door, the chick grabbed her by the waist and stuck her tongue down her throat."

"Get the fuck out of here." Brian didn't want to believe it." Was it a lesbo kiss or a—"

"It was a my-dick-got-hard-and-I-wanted-to-join-in kiss."

Brian patted his pocket and cursed when he realized he left his cigarettes in his truck.

Devon continued. "So I followed this chick and guess where she lives?"

"Brooklyn."

"Motherfucking Brooklyn. So I'm chilling in front of her apartment building, and I'm wondering what's her connection to Manny. The shit was fucking with me. About 8:35 that evening she comes out wearing a powder pink halter top with apple bottom jeans with the logo in powder pink. She had on a pair of pink high-heeled shoes with platinum-colored bottoms to match her platinum-dyed hair.

"What was the color of her lipstick?" Brian asked sarcastically.

"She wore lip gloss."

"It's good to see you pay attention to details."

Devon paid Brian no mind. "I approached her when she got to her car, and I told her that Manny wanted to speak to her. Her eyes almost popped out of her head. As soon as she opened her mouth to protest, I poked her in the ribs with my gun. I walked her to the van and threw her in the back."

Brian turned around, checking the back of the van. "Okay, so you threw her in the back of this van, I assume, and then what?"

"I drove to the factories, where the sanitation trucks park when they're not in service. There she kept denying that she knew Manny personally, said she only knew of him. I got tired of the bullshit, so I wrestled her to the floor of the van and duct taped her hands behind her back and flipped her on her stomach. I snatched her jeans down to her ankles, and she still swore she didn't know him. I grabbed a can of motor oil that was in one of the boxes in the back, and I showed it to her before ripping her panties off. The bitch cried even harder and swore to God and on her parents' graves that she didn't know Manny. But when I poured the oil down the crack of her ass, she cracked."

"She cracked?"

"Yeah, she told me where he lives, hangs out, buys his weed, everything."

"And after she told you everything you—" Brian paused for Devon to fill in the blank.

"I don't get down like that, Bee. I'll never rape a bitch."

"So you just let her go?"

"Not yet. I knocked her out and chained her to the radiator in my basement."

"Unbelievable," Brian said, shaking his head.

"I got to keep her out of sight for the rest of the night."

"Why, what's happening tonight?"

"The twins are coming by her house tonight at around 10:00 to pick her up. They're going clubbing."

"I don't care what you got to do, but you got to get that tape."

"Don't worry, Bee, it's as good as got."

Brian clasped his hands behind his head and leaned back on the headrest. "We're doing the LI spot Saturday night."

"Without Jay?"

"Without Jay and because of Jay. He's going to need a well-paid and well-connected lawyer."

"How's he doing, anyway?"

"Terrible. He's built for a lot of things, but jail ain't one of them. He's lost weight, he's scared he's gonna lose Quana, and he believes that he's gonna do a whole lot of time." Brian remembered Arlene's words and sighed. *In the game, there are no winners. Some just take a little longer to lose.* Brian opened his eyes and stared at Devon.

Devon had on a pair of black-and-grey fatigue pants with a black tank top and black Timbs. His eyes constantly darted in every direction, refusing to let any movement go unnoticed. So it didn't surprise him that Devon was the first to spot Trish a half block away walking toward them with a bag of potato chips and a Pepsi in her hand.

Devon looked at his watch. "She took thirty-seven minutes to go to the store, and all she has to show for the trip is a bag of chips and a soda? Doesn't add up."

"You love this shit, don't you?" Brian asked. "The game is a game to you. You love the excitement and the danger."

"I love it, but you eat, sleep, and breathe it," Devon countered.

"Well, I can't do it anymore. I swear on everything I love, I'm out." Brian knew that there weren't too many things he could say that would catch Devon by surprise, but he noticed how his words had a knee-jerk effect on him.

"Get the fuck out of here," Devon said in a dismissive tone. "How many times have you said you were out and days later, you would call me up with the next spot to knock?"

"A couple times."

"Seven," Devon answered. "Seven times and every time it lasted only a few days."

"I've made up my mind this time. I got a cousin living in Atlanta, and she said it's great down there, especially for raising kids."

"Denise ain't letting you take Christopher down there, and Sonia doesn't want anything to do with you."

"Sonia only has two more semesters before she gets her bachelor's degree. In the meantime, I'll be working at the hospital, stacking paper, and playing Mr. Mom. As long as she sees that I've got money and a plan, she'll go anywhere with me." Brian had been juggling the plan around in his head for the past couple days, but hearing it out loud for the first time brought a smile to his face. Sonia was the long-term planner. He was always the advocate of "live for today, for tomorrow, we'll be dead."

As Trish approached her house, Devon put on his black-and-grey fatigue jacket and pulled the Velcro straps tight and his black leather gloves.

"I got this," Brian said. "You concentrate on your date with the twins tonight."

Brian hopped out the van and made a beeline for Trish. When she saw him, she picked up her pace, trying to beat him to the front door. When she put the key into the lock, she felt Brian's hand grab her shoulder.

"Bret's not here," she said, shrugging his hand off her.

He grabbed her arm and spun her around. "Look, Trish, I'm not in the mood. Let's go."

"I'm not going anywhere with you."

Brian smacked her so hard, he jumped. "I said let's go."

He shoved her toward his truck. She began to walk, rubbing her cheek, trying not to let him see the tears welling in her eyes. When they reached the truck, he opened the door for her and slammed it behind her.

He drove without saying a word. He turned on to Linden Boulevard, heading toward Brooklyn. He really didn't know what he wanted to do with Trish.

Killing her or beating her up was out of the question. He kept cutting his eyes at her, trying to imagine her with another woman. He thought of all the nights she sat in that very seat with her head between his legs swallowing him whole. Then he pictured her munching on another woman's pussy.

When Trish realized where they were headed, she started squirming in her seat, not even bothering to hide the tears or sniffles.

Brian pulled up in front of the address Devon gave him earlier. He turned the engine off and stared straight ahead. "So how long you been seeing this chick?"

Trish cried harder.

For the first time in a long time, Brian actually had seen the sixteen year-old Trish.

"Hey," Brian said, tapping her on the back of the head, "answer the question."

"I don't know."

"What do you mean you don't know?"

"A few months maybe."

"What's a few months maybe? Three? Four? Five?"

"Five."

"When did y'all start...fondling each other?"

Trish shook her head and started crying again.

Brian tapped her in the back of the head.

"Two months ago maybe."

"When did you become a lesbo?"

"I'm not gay!" Trish said it with such force that Brian wanted to apologize.

"Okay, if you're not a lesbo, how in the world did you go from sucking dick to sucking pussy?"

"Fuck you, Brian. You don't know me. You don't know shit about me," Trish said, sobbing even louder.

"I fucking watched you grow up. How the fuck you gonna say I don't know you?"

"This isn't how it was supposed to happen."

"What was supposed to happen?"

"She said they would only come after Bret."

Brian grabbed the pack of Newports of the dashboard and lit one up. He took a long pull and exhaled real slow before he asked his next question. "What exactly was supposed to happen, Trish?"

"Ericka sat down next to me a couple months back in the school cafeteria and just started talking to me. I couldn't believe it. No one talks to me because everyone is scared of Bret. We talked, she drove me home. Every day after that, it was the same thing. We would just hang out and chitchat. One day, she wanted to go shopping, and she asked me if I wanted to come. I said, 'Sure why not?' She buys a pair of shoes and then offers to buy me a pair. She said she couldn't buy something without buying something for me. I figured it was her treat so I picked out a pair and she paid for them. From there, she would buy me perfumes, lotions, and shit like that. One day, she convinced me to come to her house so she could braid my hair. After she braided my hair, she begged me to let her put makeup on me. She took forty-five minutes to do my face. When I looked in the mirror, I couldn't believe how beautiful I was. She went into her vanity drawer and pulled out a blunt. She lit it up and took three deep pulls before handing it to me. I took a pull and choked. It wasn't pure weed in that blunt. She laughed at me and told me to take one more drag. That one drag had the room spinning. She put on some music, and she started dancing. She grabbed me and told me to dance with her. I stood up and took two steps before my legs buckled. She walked me to her bed, and I flopped down. She rubbed my arms, and I couldn't believe what I was experiencing. She was rubbing my arms, but it felt like she was rubbing my—"

"Pussy," Brian said, surprised at how she had him at the edge of his seat.

"I came so hard that when she lifted my skirt and pulled my panties to the side, I was begging her to make me cum again."

Trish put her head down, embarrassed.

Brian, being the man that he was, wanted to ask her if she ever came that hard with him, but because of the man he was, he was afraid of what the answer might be and decided not to ask. "So because she ate you out, you felt you had to return the favor?"

Trish nodded. "She made me feel so guilty when I told her that I couldn't do it. She finally convinced me to try it and...I've been doing it ever since. A couple weeks back, she told me that her cousin got killed in a robbery, a robbery that I overheard you and Bret planning the night before. I told her that Bret planned the whole thing and that he was there that night and when the guy fought back, he shot him."

Brian blinked. "You told her, knowing that they might retaliate? *Retaliate,* meaning that they would kill your brother."

"Fuck him. I don't give a fuck about him."

"You bugging, that's your brother."

"He's not my brother, he's a fucking baby-raping child molester!"

Her words hit him in the gut so hard that he almost doubled over. He replayed all the times he saw Bret and her together. How distant she looked; how she wouldn't let him touch her or get near her. Brian could feel the bile in his throat.

"I wanted him to pay for all those nights he snuck in my room and made me do all those things to him. She promised me that he would know how it felt to get fucked in the ass repeatedly."

"You mean to tell me—"

"Anything that you can think of, that bastard did to me before I reached the fifth grade."

Brian's head was spinning. His hands started shaking; and every time he tried to speak, he would stutter. Manny's words immediately came to him, "the god of kings." He had the opportunity to get half a million dollars in cash and over fifty kilos of coke.

"So you told on us, hoping that they would just come after Bret?"

"Ericka told me she would make sure that they knew that Bret was the one who shot him and that he should be the only one who should have to pay."

"This is some real Jerry Springer shit," Brian said, starting his truck. "This conversation stays between us, clear?"

Trish nodded.

"And don't worry about your brother. Niggas like him always get theirs in the end." Brian looked in his rearview mirror and saw the grey cargo van. He pulled off, smiling to himself on his way back to Queens. He gripped the steering wheel with both hands. *God,* he said to himself, *please let me make it through this weekend.*

Chapter 32

It was 1:30 p.m. according to Brian's watch. *Only thirty minutes to go,* he coached himself, *thirty more minutes before I can punch out and get the fuck out of this jumpsuit.*

Having to be at work at 6:00 a.m. every morning for the past five days was killing him. This morning, he came straight to work from the Motor Inn where he and Denise were getting drunk and high. All morning, he had been trying to define their relationship, because his relationship with her always baffled him. They were closer than brother and sister, fought like cats and dogs, and they hated the love they felt for one another. In reality, they were like night and day, but in the fabricated reality that they created with weed and Alize, they were cut from the same cloth. They had the same insecurities, weaknesses, and fears; and they both hid them well behind their short-fused anger and propensity for violence.

Last night, Brian called her, because he wanted to meet with her. He wanted to tell her that he was moving to Atlanta and getting his life together. The real reason he decided to tell her was because he knew she never bit her tongue. If she thought that it was a terrible idea, she would tell him in a heartbeat. To his surprise, she encouraged him to go. She told him that he was a straight fool and that he was going to get himself killed in New York because he's too slick for his own good. She didn't want their son growing up fatherless. They talked, smoked, and drank from midnight to 4:30 in the morning.

Now, he sat at the break table in the locker room trying to figure out how he could be in the same hotel room sitting on the same bed with the same girl he had gotten pregnant on their first and only sexual encounter and not think about sex. Even when she excused herself to go take a shower, he just laid back and thought of how he was going to make up with Sonia.

Fuck it, he thought. *The shit is giving me a head-ache. Our relationship is what it is.* He looked at his watch, it was 1:31. He felt like he was going to die. He had to make this half hour go by much faster. He walked over to the pay phone and called Devon. He got no answer. For the next half and hour, he imagined the expressions on the twins' faces when they went to pick up their friend Ericka only to find Devon there waiting for them. With each expression, he imagined, it brought a smile to his face. *I wish I could have been there,* he thought.

• • •

It was Devon's luck that Ericka's apartment was facing the street. He had a clear view of every car pulling up and driving away. He grabbed himself a sandwich and the liter bottle of Pepsi he found in the refrigerator, then sat on a chair in front of the window.

A blunt and two sandwiches later, the twins pulled up in a cherry red Volvo S60. The butterflies in his stomach started flying around. The adrenaline flowing through his veins boosted his senses to their optimal level, especially the sixth one.

Instead of getting out the car and coming up to the apartment like he thought they would, they beeped their horn. A few minutes later, the house phone rang. Devon looked at it and then back out the window. The answering machine kicked in.

"I'm not in right now, but leave a message so I can get back to you," Ericka's recorded voice sung.

Beep!

"Ericka, pick up the phone," Paula said. "I know you up there. You probably fucking that nasty nigga. Pick up, bitch."

Devon cleared his throat and picked up the phone. "Who this?"

"Who the fuck is this?"

"I guess I'm the nasty nigga."

"Where's Ericka?"

Devon put the phone down and shouted, "Yo, E, phone." He pretended like he was waiting for Ericka's response. "What? I don't know who the fuck it is." Devon picked the phone back up. "Who this?"

"Tell her it's Paula, and she better hurry up and come on."

Devon put the phone down. "It's Paula, and she said hurry the fuck up." Devon was silent for a moment. "What? Nah, fuck that. You tell the bitch yourself, I'm out of here."

"I know that nigga ain't just call me a bitch," Paula said to her sister.

Devon huffed before picking the phone up. "Yo, she said she's in the shower, and she want y'all to come up."

"Who you calling bitch, nigga?"

Devon hung up on her. As soon as he got to the window, he saw Paula crossing the street, fuming. Half walking, half running, she was coming up to confront the nasty nigga that hung up on her.

• • •

When Paula arrived in front of Ericka's door, she was breathing hard. She knocked, daring the nasty nigga to answer the door.

When the door swung open, Devon's hand locked around her neck like a bear trap, and he snatched her like a pocketbook. He reacted quicker than she could process what was happening. In one motion, he threw her face down on the couch and pinned her with his knee on her neck. He grabbed the duct tape. *One down, one to go,* he thought to himself.

Jennifer sat in the car, cursing her sister out. In her rush to get up there and confront the nigga, she had taken the phone with her. So she couldn't call up there to see what was taking them so long. She looked at her watch. Twenty minutes had passed.

For the past twenty minutes, Devon had been watching her from the window. He never lost at playing the waiting game. He watched her as she kept looking up at the apartment window while she honked the horn. Soon, she was tapping the steering wheel and talking to herself.

She's about to explode, Devon said to himself.

Just then, she snapped. Devon watched her close the windows and slam the car door. When she banged on the door, Devon took his time answering it.

Finally, he turned the knob and opened the door wide enough for her to see her sister. "Come on in, Shorty."

Jennifer jumped back.

"Whoa! Slow down, miss," Devon said. "You don't want to go running off and leave your sister here all by herself with me do you? 'Cause if you do, I promise, you'll never see her again. Alive, that is." Devon let his words sink in.

"What do you want?"

"I just want to talk."

Jennifer shook her head.

Devon walked over to the couch and put the straight razor he had gotten off of Paula that night at

Baisley Park to her neck. Jennifer slowly walked into the apartment.

Devon smiled. "Make sure you lock the door behind you."

When Jennifer locked the door, Devon motioned for her to sit on the chair he positioned by the coffee table. She walked to the chair and sat down, all the while keeping her eyes on the razor held at her sister's neck.

Devon folded the straight razor and put it in his pocket.

"We gonna make this real easy, Shorty. I'm gonna ask you one question, and you're going to answer it, and then we all go our separate ways. Understand?"

Jennifer nodded.

"Where's the videotape?"

"Manny's got it," Jennifer said.

"No shit, smart ass. Where's he got it?"

"It's in his house, but I don't know where," Jennifer said, trembling.

Devon pulled out the straight razor and unfolded it. "I thought you were going to do us all a favor and make this easy, but I guess not." He grabbed Paula's right arm and slashed her wrist.

Jennifer sprang from the chair to her sister's aid. Devon's boot connected with her stomach, knocking the wind out of her. She crumpled to the floor and watched helplessly as Devon picked up her sister's other arm and slit her other wrist.

Blood gushed from both wounds as Paula screamed into the cloth that was jammed in her mouth. She squirmed, but the duct tape wouldn't allow her to go anywhere.

Devon stood over Jennifer and grabbed her by the hair and hoisted her to her feet. He stood behind her and whispered into her ear. "Now we're gonna watch your sister bleed to death."

"The tape is in his basement. It's under a floorboard in the closet next to the pool table," Jennifer shouted.

Devon didn't move.

"I swear to God, I'm telling the truth...get off of me—"

She reached out to her sister. "Paula!"

Devon let her go and watched her fly to her sister's aid.

She ripped the sleeves of her shirt and tied them around her sister's wrist to stop the bleeding.

Devon grabbed her from behind. Jennifer clawed and kicked at him. "Get the fuck off of me."

Devon pinned her against the wall. "Listen to me very carefully. You're gonna get into your car and go get that tape."

"No! My sister—"

"And you are gonna die if you don't." Devon pointed to Paula's wrists. "You stopped the bleeding, she'll be okay for now."

Devon let her go.

Jennifer looked at him and then back to her sister.

"You better hurry," Devon said.

Jennifer took off, she hopped in her car and sped off.

Devon walked over to Paula, folding and unfolding the straight razor. "Word on the street is when the cops found Supreme in the hotel room, they found him with his dick in his mouth. That shit is gangsta." Devon shook his head. "I got to know. Which of you bitches did it?"

Paula's eyes answered his question.

Devon nodded. "Cool."

• • •

Brian punched out at two o'clock on the dot. "Yo, Kenny, I'm out of here, see you Monday."

"You must have a hot date, the way you bolting out of here."

"Nah, I'm just trying to get away from your gay ass. I heard that shit's contagious."

"Negro, please. I'm not even going to feed into that."

"Wow, that's a first for you."

"Yeah, whatever."

Brian grabbed his duffle bag and headed out. When he got into his truck, he reached into his glove compartment and pulled out his cell phone. There were no messages from Sonia. He swallowed his pride and dialed her number. She picked up on the fourth ring.

"What?" she said, irritated.

"Sweetheart," Brian said, "listen."

Click!

When she hung up on him, he smiled like he'd just won the lotto. When Sonia didn't want anything to do with him, she would avoid his calls at all costs. When she started calming down, she would answer the phone and let him say a couple words before hanging up. *By tomorrow,* he thought, *she let me apologize before hanging up.*

Brian tried calling Devon one more time. He was caught off guard when he answered.

"What up?"

"I've been calling you all day," Brian said. "Did you get the tape?" "No doubt."

Brian hit his dashboard. "That's what I'm talking about! I don't care what anybody says about you. You are the motherfucking man."

"Yeah, and that's not all."

"Aw shit, here comes the bad news."

"I wouldn't call it bad news."

"What is it?"

"Paula—"

"One of the twins, right?"

"Yeah, well, remember when Jay told us that he had heard that when the police found Supreme, they found him with his dick in his mouth?"

"Yeah."

"She did it."

"Get the fuck out of here."

"Nah, Bee. She did that. So I called a friend of mine, and he gave me Chuka's cell phone number. I called him up and told him I had some information for him."

Everybody knows that the last place anybody saw Supreme was at the Dynasty, so I took a picture of Paula with my phone and sent it to his phone. I told him to show it around the club and see if anybody seen her with Supreme that night. The nigga called me back half an hour later, on fire. He said one of the girls recognized her and said she was definitely with Supreme that night. The chick said she was sure because there were two of them, twins."

"So I told Chuka that Manny was behind the whole thing."

"You slick motherfucker," Brian said. "That's that art of war shit. 'The enemy of my enemy is my friend.'"

"Fuck it, why not let Chuka take care of him."

"No doubt," Brian said.

"So to make a long story short, he comes to Ericka's apartment where I got the twins duct taped. He questions them and when he's convinced that they are telling the truth, he pulls out his nine and shoots Paula in the head. I grabbed his arm, but his gun was already pointed at Jennifer's chest. He squeezed off a shot before I wrestled him to the ground."

Brian realized that he was holding his breath.

"We rolled around, on the floor, cursing at each other, but I got to my feet first and got the gun. He got up slowly and told me that he owed it to Supreme to take both them bitches out. He dusted himself off and told me that Manny would be dead before the weekends out."

Brian exhaled. "This shit is getting out of hand, Dev. In all our time together, we never seen this much bloodshed."

"It was bound to happen."

"What about Ericka, the chick in your basement?"

"What chick in my basement?"

Brian's hand trembled when he reached for his pack of cigarettes. "Are you going to be able to do this tomorrow night, Dev?"

"It's a piece of cake."

"I mean, with all the shit you went through today and all."

"Let me know where to meet you."

When Devon hung up, Brian was lighting his second cigarette.

Chapter 33

One thirty, Saturday afternoon, Brian pulled up in front of the strip club. The Closed sign was hanging, but Brian knew better. He knocked on the window until the bartender came running from the back.

"You trying to break my window, motherfucker?"

Brian brushed past him and headed to the back. Knowledge and Skillz were both sitting in a corner booth, talking to a stripper, who Brian remembered from the week before. It was hard to forget a woman who could puff a cigarette with her pussy.

When Knowledge saw him, he pulled a few bills out his pocket and put it in the girl's hand. He smacked her on the ass as she got up and walked toward the door that said employees only.

"What up, Born?" Skillz said, getting up to meet Brian halfway.

"Same shit, different smell."

"Yo, Al," Knowledge screamed out to the bartender, "bring my man a Heineken."

They all sat at the booth, silent, until Al brought the Heineken and left. Knowledge was the first to speak.

"So how we gonna do this?"

Brian twisted the cap off the Heineken bottle and took a long drink. He looked at the bottle as if he was reading the ingredients, and then he burped. "It's real simple. According to Skillz here, the only shot we got into getting into that house is when they order pizza."

"Nah," Skillz said, "niggas be on point. When the delivery dude shows up, them niggas be right on the other side of the door, guns cocked."

Brian shook his head. "You ever heard of the Trojan horse?"

"No doubt," Skillz said. "I got one in my wallet right now."

"He ain't talking about the condom, god," Knowledge said. "Over three thousand years ago, the Trojans took one of the Greeks females, she was supposed to be some hot chick that everybody wanted to fuck, so the Greeks went to the Trojan's city of Troy and tried to break in to their fortress, but they couldn't. They fought for like ten years."

"Ten fucking years over a bitch?" Skillz said.

"You know how them crackers are," Knowledge said.

"Yeah, ten years," Brian continued. "Finally, someone came up with the idea to build a gigantic wooden horse as a gift for the Trojans. Only this horse would be full of soldiers. The plan was when they brought the horse into the fortress, the soldiers would come out at night and attack them from the inside out."

"Aye, yo, that's some ill shit right there," Skillz said, hitting the table. "But how's that shit gonna work for us?"

Brian pointed at him. "You're gonna order pizza. Only when you call, you'll be calling this disposable cell phone I picked up yesterday. You give me the order, I go into Dominos and grab the order." Brian reached into his pants pocket and pulled out a clear bottle. "This is liquid morphine. I'm gonna pour this into the sodas that you're gonna make sure they order."

In about four hours, they'll be knocked out.

"That's when you'll blink the lights to let me and Knowledge know that we can bust up in there."

"Okay, when they out, I blink the lights, and then let y'all in."

"No!" Brian said. "We'll come around the back with the battering ram and smash the backdoor in. It has to look like somebody busted up in there."

"Yeah, yeah, no doubt," Skillz said.

Knowledge looked at his watch. "Time for you to break out little nigga."

Skillz looked at his Rolex. "Oh shit, it's 2:30. I'm out, peace." Skillz swallowed the last of his drink and took off.

"So what are we going to do until he makes that call?" Knowledge asked.

"We just sit tight and wait. That's the hardest part."

• • •

"Aye, yo, Skillz, roll some more of that shit up," Fat Tommy said as he finished off the last of his blunt.

"Damn, nigga," Skillz said. "You got three other niggas up in here trying to smoke too, fat motherfucker."

"Y'all niggas don't want to smoke. Y'all too busy fucking with that PlayStation."

T-Black and Cream looked up from the screen. T-Black got on him first. "Won't you go find something to do?"

"Yeah," Cream jumped in. "Order us some food, you fat bitch."

Skillz jumped. "Whoa, that's a good idea. Let me take care of that."

Cream looked at him. "Okay, order some chicken and—"

"Nah," T-Black said, "we eat chicken every fucking night."

"I'm gonna order...pizza," Skillz said.

"I had pizza just before I walked into this bitch," Tommy said.

Skillz started getting nervous. "I don't give a fuck what you had. You probably had a little bit of everything before you got here."

"I don't want no fucking pizza either," T-Black said. "As a matter of fact, let's get some Chinese food."

"Yeah, Chinese food," Tommy said.

"Sounds like a plan to me," Cream said.

"Call them up, Skillz."

Skillz was stuck. He pictured Born delivering Chinese food to the house.

"The fuck you waiting on, nigga?" Tommy yelled at him.

Skillz opened up his phone and dialed the number Brian gave him earlier.

• • •

Brian answered on the third ring.

"Dominos, can I take your order?"

"Yeah, I would like—"

Brian heard the three dudes in the background yelling out their orders.

Skillz spoke into the phone. "Three, no, four pints of beef fried rice, and—"

"What the fuck are you talking about, Skillz?" Brian said.

"Yeah, and five egg rolls, and four half a chicken, and a three liter bottle of soda. You got that?"

"You were supposed to be ordering pizza, Skillz. Fucking pizza!" Brian screamed in the phone.

"They outvoted me," he whispered into the phone. "Niggas wanted Chinese food."

"We'll be there in thirty minutes." Brian sighed and put him on hold.

"What's up?" Knowledge asked.

"They ordered Chinese."

"How the fuck we gonna pull that off?"

Brian grabbed a napkin and wrote down their order. "Here, go and pick this up. I'll take care of the rest." Brian called Skillz back on his cell. "What up?"

"Listen to me. Make sure you're the one at the door getting the shit, because the bottle of soda is going to be open. I got to crack it so I can dump the morphine in, got it?"

"Got it."

• • •

Thirty minutes later, Brian pulled up in the stolen Jeep Cherokee. Knowledge was slumped down on the passenger's side floor.

Brian got out with the Chinese food and headed toward the house. Before he reached the top of the steps, the door cracked open.

Brian called out nonchalantly, "Chinese food." Brian could hear whispering behind Skillz. He heard someone say "What the fuck?"

The owner of the voice yanked Skillz out the way and opened the door. "Since when black people started delivering Chinese food?" T - Black asked.

"Since the Chinese motherfuckers got tired of getting robbed by black people." Brian heard someone laugh in the background. T-Black eyed him for a moment.

Brian played the game. "Do you want it or not?" When T-Black didn't respond, he turned to walk away.

"Hold up, nigga," Tommy said, coming from behind the door. "Let me get that." T-Black stared him down.

Tommy stared back at him. "What, nigga? I'm hungry, and you playing games."

That was Skillz cue. "Look out," he said grabbing the food and soda, "all you motherfuckers are playing games." He turned to Tommy. "Pay the god."

Tommy handed Brian twenty-five dollars and told him to keep the change. When Tommy slammed the door, Brian walked back to the jeep, drove to the corner, and parked. Knowledge looked up before sitting up.

Brian looked at his watch, it was 6:30 p.m. "Well, we should be on in about four hours." He reclined his seat and closed his eyes.

"You just gonna go to sleep?" Knowledge asked.

"You got a faster way to pass the time?"

Knowledge reclined his seat and laid back, but he didn't go to sleep. Neither did Brian.

• • •

At 10:30 on the dot, Brian and Knowledge saw the lights blink off and on.

Brian parked across the street from the house.

Knowledge grabbed the duffle bag from the backseat.

Brian got out and grabbed the duffle bag and the battering ram.

They ran to the back of the house with ski masks on and listened. Knowledge held the screen door open and watched Brian fly full force into the backdoor with the battering ram. To his surprise, the door buckled on the first attempt.

Skillz came rushing into the kitchen and almost got a bullet in the head. He stared down the barrel of Brian's fo'fif.

"Easy, god."

"Where they at?" Brian asked.

"They all in the living room knocked the fuck out, yo."

Brian walked into the living room and checked on them. They looked like they were going to sleep for hours.

Brian looked at his watch. "C'mon, let's do this. We ain't got too much time before the shift change."

Skillz took them to the bedroom where the stash was. He moved the bed and knocked on the floor. It was hollow.

Brian reached down and pulled the floor up. The expression on his face didn't change, but his heart rate did. He'd never see so much money or drugs in his life. Knowledge was wearing a smile from shoulder to shoulder. He was definitely impressed.

As planned, Brian scooped up the stacks of money and stuffed them into his duffle bag. Knowledge grabbed the kilos of coke and stacked them in his duffle bag.

"Yo, Skillz," Knowledge called out. "All this ain't gonna fit in this bag. Go get me a garbage bag."

"Just carry what you can, we ain't got that much time left," Brian said.

"Fuck that. I ain't going through all this just to leave some shit behind." Skillz came back with the garbage bag and watched Knowledge put the rest of the kilos in it.

Brian tossed his duffle bag over his shoulder with a grunt. *This shit got to weight a least fifty pounds,* he thought to himself.

When they got to the living room, Brian stopped and pulled out a needle filled with morphine.

Skillz looked at him. "Who's that for?"

"It's for you. They got to find you doped up just like them. If not, they're gonna know you had something to do with the robbery."

"Nah," Skillz said. "I'll take my chances. I'll just tell the boss I was asleep when these motherfuckers ordered out, and when I woke up, I found these niggas like this."

"That ain't gonna work," Brian said.

"You sticking me with that needle ain't gonna work either."

Bang!

Brian jumped when he heard the gun go off. As he reached for his gun, Knowledge was putting his away. Brian cursed himself for sleeping on Knowledge. He looked at him and shook his head.

"What the fuck you want me to do?" Knowledge asked. "You said we got to get out of here, right? And this motherfucker was playing games."

"He was just a kid."

"Ain't no such thing in this game, god."

A pool of blood started to gather around Skillz's head.

Knowledge looked down at him; the vulture flew out of him. He bent down and pulled the Rolex off Skillz's wrist. He snatched his platinum chain. Knowledge started taking the jewelry off of the other dudes and digging through their pockets as well.

"What the fuck are you doing? We got duffle bags full of money and drugs and you taking twenty dollar bills out of these niggas' pockets?"

"Got to make it look like a robbery, right?"

Brian looked at his watch. "It's 10:48, we got to go before the next shift drives up."

• • •

They exited the house through the back door. As they walked to the head of the driveway, Brian heard an engine accelerating. Brian and Knowledge pulled out their guns and opened fire on the Acura that was bearing down on them. The car skidded to a stop; Brian and Knowledge ran toward the jeep.

One of the occupants in the Acura jumped out with a machine gun in hand and turned Knowledge into Swiss cheese.

Brian slid behind the jeep as a hail of bullets hit the spot he just occupied a fraction of a second ago. He peeked over the hood of the jeep and saw Knowledge, face down in the middle of the street. His body spurting blood. He ducked as the kid with the machine gun opened fire.

Brian heard the back windshield shatter as he ejected his empty clip and put in a fresh one. When he peeked back over the hood, all four were out of the car armed and pointing their guns at him. He squeezed off two shots before twenty came at him.

The four dudes knew they had him pinned. So they took their time approaching him. Brian looked up and saw when they split up. Two ran up on the sidewalk across from him, and the other two ran up on the sidewalk he was on.

The two on his side quickened their pace, confident that they had him outnumbered and outgunned. It was their confidence that caused them not to see Devon slide from the side of the house they just ran by. He pointed the two Uzis at them and cut them down like trees.

The other two, shocked, turned toward Devon and opened fire. Brian used the time Devon bought him to take aim and fire. His first bullet hit one of the dudes in the arm. The dude screamed as his arm fell to his side, lifeless. His second shot just missed the other guy's head. He ducked down and stayed down.

Devon walked into the middle of the street toward Knowledge. *Devon, what the fuck are you doing?* Brian said to himself.

Devon yanked the blood-stained duffle bag off of Knowledge's shoulder, then picked up the garbage bag. Brian kept his gun trained on the last dude, daring him to pop his head up.

Devon climbed into the Jeep Cherokee and started it up. Brian jumped in and fired three shots as Devon peeled off. The lone gunman shot after them, but he was out of range to hit anything.

When Devon turned the corner, he jumped out. Brian followed him to a black Pontiac Grand Am. They hopped in and headed back to Queens.

"I told you my plan was better," Devon said.

Earlier, before Brian had pulled up to the strip club, Devon didn't feel right about putting all their eggs in one basket, meaning, if he and Brian were together and they both got into trouble, who would bail them out? That's how they always did it. Either he or Jay would always play the shadows so that they could take care of the unexpected.

"Yeah," Brian said. "You were right once again, my friend."

"So how much you think is in them bags?"

"I don't know, but it sure looked like there was more than fifty kilos and five hundred thousand." Brian laughed out loud.

"What's so funny?" Devon asked.

"I can tell you exactly how much money and drugs there are."

"How much?"

"Bret said there would be half a million and fifty kilos."

"Yeah."

"Half a million and fifty kilos was his cut. The duffle bag that I gave Knowledge could hold fifty kilos easy. He had to get a garbage bag to put the other half in."

"The other half?"

Brian opened his cell phone and called Andrea. "I'll be there in fifteen minutes." He hung up and smiled. "I'm willing to bet that we have at least a million dollars in cash back there."

Devon nodded. "Cool."

Chapter 34

Brian dumped the duffle bag of money on Andrea's basement floor. It took him and Devon fifteen minutes to count it.

"Nine hundred and fifty thousand," Brian said, astonished.

They moved to the duffle bag and garbage bag of coke and dumped them on the floor. They stacked the kilos in stacks of ten. They had eight rows with eight left over.

"Eighty eight," Devon said, astonished. "How much of this are you giving to Bret?"

"We ain't giving him shit."

Devon looked at him.

Brian related the story that Trish told him about her brother.

By the time Brian finished the story, Devon was ready to take him right then.

"I say we do that nigga tonight," Devon said.

"Nah, what we got to concentrate on now is getting Jay a lawyer and making sure Chuka takes care of that business with Manny."

When Devon heard the door to the basement open, he ran up the steps and blocked Andrea from coming down.

"Get out of my way. This is my fucking house."

Devon didn't budge.

Andrea tried to push by him, but Devon was an impenetrable wall. Even her eyesight couldn't get past him.

Brian ran up the steps because he could see Devon putting her through the wall with no problem.

"I got this, Dev. Go and bag that shit up so we can get out of here." Devon spun around and headed back downstairs.

"I can't stand him," Andrea said. "He makes me sick."

"He's in love with you."

"Please, don't make me vomit."

"I'm for real. He told me that if he ever found out that I wasn't hitting that ass right, he was going to take you from me and treat you like a woman."

"Well, you're hitting this ass the way it loves to be hit so tell pit bull down there he need not worry."

"That's what I told him. Besides, you don't want to be treated like a woman anyway." Brian said, smiling.

"Fuck you."

Just hearing the word *fuck* come out of Andrea's mouth did something to him. He looked past her toward the living room. She must have read his mind, because she smiled and started rubbing the bulge in his pants.

Brian pulled back. "Not now. I got something to do."

"It won't take but five minutes, big daddy," she said as she gently bit his bottom lip.

Fuck it, Brian thought. *It will only take me a minute.*

Just then, Devon walked to the bottom of the steps.

"I took care of that, Bee."

Brian could have taken the look that Andrea gave Devon and put a handle on it and slice through steel.

Brian pulled back from Andrea. "I'll meet you in the car."

Devon walked up the steps, never taking his eyes off of Andrea, even as he passed her and headed out the door.

Brian grabbed Andrea by the hand and led her down into the basement. He pointed at the two duffle bags and garbage bag. "I need you to hold this down here for a few days."

He picked up the bags and put them in the cedar closet.

"How much money is in there?"

"Don't worry about that. Just make sure nothing happens to it."

As Brian walked up the steps, Andrea held on to his back pants pockets. He knew she wasn't going to let him leave without giving her some of the magic stick. When they got to the top of the steps, he turned around.

"Two minutes, Andrea."

She turned around and bent over at the waist as she pulled down her jeans and thongs in one motion. "Two minutes, Daddy. I promise."

• • •

Manny sat on the plush hotel couch, bare chest, relaxed. He had just gotten all of the stress and tenseness of the streets drained from him. For the past hour, he had his dick sucked and asshole reamed by the "newest edition" to his stable, a young white chick with the ass and hips of Mother Africa. He was still "breaking her in," as he liked to call it, which meant, when he got tired of her, he would unleash her to the world of hustlers and thugs.

Earlier, he got word that Freeze was trying to discreetly inquire about his whereabouts. Discreet and street rhymed but they went together like oil and water. Word got back to Manny faster than a pregnancy test.

Ordinarily, he would hunt a nigga down immediately, throwing him off guard, and if the nigga ain't have a good reason for inquiring about him, that was a good enough reason for Manny to put the lame out of his misery. Not this time though. Freeze's inquiries and the twins' sudden disappearance yesterday had one thing in common—Chuka. Everybody knew Freeze was not only head of Brooklyn's most notori-

ous gang, but he was also the eyes, ears, and sometimes mouthpiece for Chuka.

With Tequan dead, it was only a matter of time
before niggas started trying to make their claim as
king of the hill. Manny lit the half a blunt that was
lying in the ashtray and imagined the length niggas
would be willing to go to take Tequan's place. As usual,
he would sit back and watch the free-for-all. And as
usual, he would appear when the dust cleared and
the blood dried, and the new king of the hill will have
no choice but to employ his services.

Manny was like the J. Edgar Hoover of the game.
He had life destroying dirt on everybody, from niggas
who smoked crack on the low to the niggas who were
sucking dick, on the super down low. He laughed at
the last thought. Tequan was what the streets called
a "homo thug." He had more heart than a lot of the
super niggas Manny knew, but long black dick was
his kryptonite. Kryptonite that Manny used cunningly
to achieve lifetime employment with Tequan. If Chuka
wanted to be king of the hill, Manny had no problem
with that because he had more dirt on him than a
shark has teeth.

The Grand Hyatt was a hotel that Manny went to
when he wanted to get away from the streets. Of all
the places he could go, he always came to the Grand
Hyatt. It held a lot of memories for him. His mother
used to work here changing the linen. When he turned
eighteen, she got him a job there as well. He immediately saw how the establishment treated the white

employees different from the black slaves. He quit two days later. He couldn't believe that his mother had put up with it for over ten years. She put up with it for another ten years. After which, they laid her off, blaming it on cutbacks. Now, here he was twelve years later, after his mother's death, imagining how many times his mother must have came into this very suite and collected some cracker's shitty cum-stained sheets.

The hotel phone rang. He picked it up on the fifth ring.

"Hello?"

"Yes, Mr. Rohan. Your food is on the way up."

"Is the steak medium rear like I requested?"

"Yes, sir."

"You said, 'yes, sir,' fifteen minutes ago, and the motherfucker was raw. I look like a fucking animal to you?"

"No, sir I—"

"If the shit ain't medium rare, I'm sending it back down."

Manny hung up. The first steak was medium rare just the way he like it, but he had to fuck with them. It was his way of getting payback for his mother.

When room service brought his food, he tasted the steak and thought about sending it back just for spite, but he didn't want to chance it. Next time they brought it up, it may have some "special sauce" hawked on it.

He wheeled the cart of food in and slammed the door in the server's face. When he heard the server mumble something under his breath, he swung the door open.

"Excuse me, what did you say?"

The server's face turned white. "Nothing, sir. I was just—"

Manny slammed the door in his face again. He rolled the cart to the dinning table, smiling. He looked up at the ceiling. "That one was for you, Ma."

• • •

Brian and Devon dumped the jeep at the Long Island Railroad's Rosedale Train Station. They walked up the block to Devon's Land Rover and headed to Laquana's house.

Brian called her cell phone, but she wasn't answering. When they pulled up in front of the house, all the lights were out.

"Let's just come back in the morning, Bee."

"Nah, fuck that. Wait here." Brian got out the truck and walked around into the backyard. He picked up a handful of pebbles and threw them at Laquana's window one by one.

Finally, her light came on. She came to the window and opened it. "Boy, you crazy, coming here this late?" Laquana whispered.

"I need to talk to you, it's important."

Laquana sucked her teeth and closed the window. That meant she would be down in five minutes.

Five minutes later, she unlocked the patio door and stepped outside in her robe and slippers. She folded her arms and shifted her weight to her right hip. "What?"

"How's Jay doing?"

Laquana rolled her eyes. "I can't believe you got me out of bed to ask me how that trifling ass nigga is doing."

"Actually," Brian started, "I wanted to know how you were doing." Laquana turned her head.

"Did you work that shit out with Teshawna?"

"She's gone."

"Gone?"

"Called her mother up and told her she wanted to come home. So my pops brought her a bus ticket, and she broke the fuck out."

"So back to the original question. How you doing?"

"I don't know how I'm doing, Brian. I love my cousin to death. I raised her. I changed her diapers, taught her ABCs, and everything. And then for her to do what she did really...tore me up inside." Laquana's eyes were brimming with tears, but she refused to let them fall.

Brian could see Laquana's folded arms slowly soften into a hug. He walked to her, and without a word, he hugged her. Her arms wrapped around him like a vise grip. Finally, she gave her tears permission to fall.

Brian knew Laquana since the first grade. He remembered the first day he met her.

His pops had finally got the loan from the army he was always fussing about. As he promised, he was going to move his family—which at the time only consisted of Brian, his little brother, and his mother—out of the slums of Manhattan and into the suburbs of Queens. Brian was six years old.

On the first day of school, his pops introduced him to an ugly bony girl who was shorter than him but two years his senior. Her name was Laquana, and it was her job to make sure that li'l Brian made it to the bus stop to and from school every day. For the next five years, everybody made fun of the ugly duckling, including li'l Brian. But the ugly duckling had the last laugh, because one day out of the blue, the ugly duckling had become a swan, a curvaceous swan. All the boys, and even some girls, wanted to taste that honey. Not Brian though. He refused to look at her as beautiful. Not because she wasn't, but he knew if he fell to her feet like the other kids, she would treat him like the rest. He wasn't the rest. He knew her when she was bony and had stink breath, and he always reminded her of that through the years. Of course, Laquana knew better. That was just Brian's way of telling her that he loved her like a sister. Even now, as he hugged her, she could feel the love emanating from him.

Brian held her for a couple more minutes before speaking. "I need two favors from you, Quana."

She looked up at him. "What's that?"

"You're the only one I know who has a large sum of money in the bank, and you have excellent credit."

"And?"

"And I want you to take out a loan."

"How much?"

"Eighty thousand."

"Eighty thousand? You out of you're fucking mind?" she shouted loud enough for the dead to hear.

"Damn, baby girl. Why don't you just wake everybody up and tell them our business?"

"I can't get no loan for eighty thousand."

"Yes, you can, I know you can."

"What you need it for?"

"I came into some money. A lot of money, and I just can't go around throwing thousands around without being noticed. So I need you to get the loan and agree to pay it back over a period of five years. I will give you a hundred and twenty up front."

"A hundred and twenty thousand?"

"Yeah, I'm figuring the most they'll charge you is 12 percent interest. So of the hundred and twenty thousand, you got to pay them roughly ninety thousand, and you're left with thirty thousand for yourself."

"You serious?"

Brian dug into his pocket and counted out ten Gs and handed it to her. "That's for you to do what you want."

"Who'd you kill to get this?"

He didn't know if she said that in a joking manner or if she was dead serious.

"I ain't have to kill anyone." Brian watched her as she put the money in her robe pocket.

"What's the second favor?" she asked.

"I'm going to need you to go to Weinstein's office and take half of the eighty and retain his legal services for Jay?"

Quana stopped stuffing her pockets.

"Don't say a word, Quana. I know what he did was wrong. He's a dog. I'll admit that, but look at it from my angle. He's my man, and I can't just sit back and watch my man get twenty-five to life. He's not built for prison, Quana."

"Nigga, you ain't got to convince me. The thirty thousand and the ten you just gave me was good enough," Laquana said, smiling.

"It's good to see you smile."

"Money has a way of bringing the best out of me."

Brian gave her a hug before turning to leave. "Come Monday morning. Make sure you start the loan process."

"Nigga, please. I'm gonna fill the paperwork out online tomorrow morning. You just make sure you bring my money."

"Love ya, Q."

"Bring my money, nigga."

• • •

Manny jumped out of his sleep when he heard his cell phone ringing. He looked at the clock on the night stand. It was 12:30 in the morning. He picked up his phone.

"Yo!"

"Yo, Manny. It's Kendu. I'm at King's County Hospital. Jennifer's in the intensive care unit."

Manny perked up. "What happened?"

"Paula is dead, yo. Detectives found them up in an apartment, shot up."

Kendu was the twin's cousin, so Manny had to pretend like he really cared. "I'm sorry, man. That's really fucked up. I don't know what to say."

"Jennifer's asking to talk to you. She's saying it's real important."

"Yeah, okay. I'll be there in the morning."

"Nah, she wants to see you now. Something about them having the videotape or something."

Manny jumped out of the bed and started getting dress as he held the phone to his ear. "How am I going to get in there to see her, it's 12:30 in the morning?"

"I already hooked it up with the doctor on the night shift. I told him that you are her uncle, and that we're her only family."

"I'll be there in about half an hour."

When Kendu hung up, he felt the pressure of the 9mm nudged against his head lighten.

"You did good, homie," Chuka said from the backseat of the SUV.

"If Manny finds out that I set him up, he'll kill me."

"Don't worry. He won't live to find out. And if you want to continue living, you and your cousin who's lying up in there, you'll keep your mouth shut, feel me?"

Kendu nodded.

Chuka decided not to finish Jennifer off. He believed that when people have near-death experiences, they change their whole lives around for the better. *Besides, she would be an example,* Chuka thought, *an example of my wrath and my mercy. Niggas can never say I ain't never show no one mercy.*

Chuka spoke to the driver. "Put the others on point. Scrams will be here in a half hour."

• • •

Brian called Sonia just as Devon pulled up in front of her house.

"Hello"

"What you doing up?" Brian said.

Click!

Brian dialed her number again.

"It's too late to be playing this game, Brian."

"Listen, I'm right in front of the house. Come outside so we can talk.

"No!"

"I'm gonna walk up to your front door and knock real loud until I wake your parents up, and then I'm gonna tell them how bad you've been treating me."

"Fuck you, Brian." Sonia hung up.

"I'm gonna get out here, Dev."

"You sure?"

"Yeah, we got some shit to work out. Keep in contact with your man to see if Chuka took care of that unfinished business."

"I'll stay on it."

Brian headed to the house as Devon took off. He didn't want to knock on Mr. Ingram's door at 1:00 in the morning. He didn't even want to knock on it at 1:00 in the afternoon. So he prayed that Sonia wouldn't call his bluff. He ran up the steps with every intention of not knocking.

His heartbeat raced as he got to the door and didn't see Sonia's face at the front door. His fear quickly turned to anger. *Who the fuck did she think she was dealing with? She was playing him like he was some young punk trying to take her out on the money he saved from his paper route. Now, he had every intention on knocking; and if Mr. Ingram came to the door, he would curse him and anybody else out who came outside.* As he opened the screen door, Sonia opened the front door.

Brian shouted into the house. "Who you think you fucking with?"

Sonia quickly pushed him outside and shut the door behind her. "Why you yelling? Calm down."

"Nah! Fuck that! I'm tired of you playing me like I'm some fucking punk. Every time we have an argument, I got to walk on eggshells and wait for you to calm down so we can talk. I got to go and buy you all kinds of shit to say I'm sorry, even if you were the one who started it. You hang up on me time and time again. And what do I do? I call you back. I'm the one always trying to make up, trying to make shit work, while you give me this pissy attitude. I'm tired of dealing with it." Brian turned and walked down the steps.

Sonia ran down the steps and cut in front of him. "Okay, okay."

"No, it's not okay. Move." Brian pushed her to the side and continued walking 'til she ran in front of him again.

"Okay, Brian. You made your point."

Brian shook his head. "Look at you. You can't even say it." Sonia put her head down. Brian walked past her.

Sonia cut in front of him and shoved him. "All right. I'm—"

Sonia clenched her fist at her sides. "I'm...sorry. You happy now? I said it."

"No, I'm not happy. That's not what I want to hear. 'I'm sorry for being such a bitch, Brian.' That's what I want to hear."

Sonia put her hands on her hips. Brian could see the smoke coming out of her flaring nostrils.

"I'm sorry," Brian said, coaching her.

"I'm sorry for being...for being such a...bitch," Sonia said through clenched teeth.

Brian walked up to her and tilted his head down 'til it was touching hers. "We're gonna get something straight, right here tonight. I'm the man of this relationship, the head." He nudged her head with his. "So you will treat me like I'm the motherfucking man. Understand?"

Sonia nodded weakly.

"I said, do you understand?" Brian yelled in her face.

Sonia pushed him. "Yes, I understand."

"Well, then fucking act like it."

They walked back to Sonia's house and sat on the front porch. Brian told her how he wanted to move to Atlanta or anywhere down south after she graduated. Everything he talked about was geared toward the benefit of the baby. He knew she would be more open if she thought he was looking out for their best interest, and he was right. He promised to talk to her about it more in the morning. He gave her a kiss and headed on home. On his way, he thought of all the businesses he was going to open when he got down there. *I'll be a millionaire before I'm twenty five,* he thought. *Fuck being the god of kings, I'm about to be god, period."*

● ● ●

When Manny pulled up to the red light across the street from the hospital, a car speeding from the other side of the street swerved and hit him head on.

His airbag popped out with a loud bang, disorienting him. When he opened his eyes, the three gunmen standing at the side of his car opened fire. In a matter of seconds, Manny became five pounds of lead heavier.

The gunmen backed off when they saw Chuka walking up with machete in hand. With one swipe, he separated Manny's head from his body. He made sure he did it in plain view of Kendu. Chuka's message was simple, "Death was only the beginning of his wrath." God himself couldn't get Kendu to ever rat on him.

Chapter 35

Two weeks later, right after work, Brian went to Rikers Island to see Jay. Brian barely recognized the toothpick in the grey jumpsuit walking toward him.

"What the fuck, Jay? You smoking crack up in here?"

"I'm smoking, but it ain't crack. You got to stay treed up in here, you know?"

"Yeah, I hear you. Niggas ain't charging you an arm and a leg for the shit, are they?"

"I get my own shit. Remember Nicole?"

"Swallow you whole Nicole?"

"Yeah, that bitch. She be coming through to check a nigga. She be bringing me trees and sending me pictures of her in sexy lingerie to jerk off to and shit like that." He slumped down in the chair. "She ain't no Quana though. I miss the hell out of her, Bee. I can't eat. I can't sleep. She was the best thing to ever happen to me. I thought when she found out about me and her cousin that she would never talk to me again, but when you told me she took out that loan and got the lawyer for me, I knew there was hope for us. I swear, Bee, on everything I love, I'm gonna treat her right when I beat this."

Laquana got the loan for Brian as she said she would. She even went to Mr. Weinstein's office and paid him the ten thousand retainer he asked for, but she made it crystal clear to him that she was doing it for him. As far as she was concerned, if Jason would have got ganged-raped his throat cut, she wouldn't lose a moment's rest. She patched things up with her cousin. After all, they were family, and no matter how Laquana looked at it, it boiled down to one thing. Jason knew she was young and naïve. He was the one who took advantage.

Brian didn't want to tell him that Laquana was over him and had moved on to someone else. She was also planning on going away to college in September. So he did what he does best, he changed the subject.

"And when you get out, you ain't never got to work. We straight for life."

Jason forgot about Laquana. "Yo, I still can't believe y'all did it, Bee. Of all the ones to miss, I missed the score that set us straight for life. Damn, I wish I could have been there."

"Look on the bright side. You're going to be there to spend that paper."

"No doubt." Jason looked around and lowered his voice. "Y'all ain't get rid of all that coke yet?"

"Nah, we taking the turtle express on that. We don't want the streets knowing we got it like that. Word may get back to Long Island, you know?"

"Yeah, yeah. No doubt. I got to give it to you and Dev, y'all got patience like a motherfucker. I would have sold that shit that same night I got my hands on it."

"And you would have spent all the money you made from it the next day."

"You damn right."

"That's why you're not the brains of the operations, nigga."

It was Jason's turn to change the subject. "That's fucked up about what happened to Bret."

Jason was referring to last week Thursday when Bret's mom found him in his room, dead. Apparently, he overdosed on the heroin he shot into his veins. The needle was still in his arm when she found him.

"Yeah," Brian said. "That's fucked up."

"Fuck it. Look on the bright side, you ain't have to give him shit."

Yeah, Brian thought. *I ain't have to give him nothing but that hot shot in the arm, while Dev held him down.*

The CO walked over to the table. "Time's up."

"Damn, that was quick," Brian said.

"Yeah, time flies when you're having fun," Jason said regaining some of his humor. "Yo, Bee, talk to Quana for me. Try to get her up here to see a nigga. Let her know I changed."

"Let's stay focused on this trial, Jay. She'll be there."

"Nah, Bee. I don't think so. I heard she's fucking with some high yellow nigga named Lyte. Did you know that?"

Brian's throat was drier than the Sahara Desert. "Know what?"

"Don't fuck with me, Bee. You was never a good liar."

"I wouldn't say she's fucking with him like fucking him. I think she just needs to start going out again. And I'm gonna be honest with you. I think it's doing her some good. She would just sleep all day and night. She was one miserable bitch. She almost lost her job behind losing you to the penitentiary."

Brian grabbed his bony shoulder. "She'll be there when you get there, Jay."

"What if that nigga gets into her head, and she flips on me? What if she gets pregnant by the nigga? What if—"

Brian could see the panic in his eyes. Patience was never one of Jason's attributes.

"I got to get out of here before that nigga gets into her head, Bee. I need you to call the lawyer and ask him what's up. I wrote the motherfucker like five times, and he ain't respond yet. Dude came to see me once to introduce himself and that was it."

"I got you. Don't even sweat it. I'm gonna call him when I get home."

The CO was quickly making his rounds back to their table. Brian stood up. The last time the CO hand to tell him twice, they punished Jason for it. All the sticky pages out of the *Don Diva* magazines that he brought up for Jason to read were mysteriously ripped out.

"All right, Jay. I'm out."

They both rose and gave each other a hug.

"Keep you head up, Jay. We gonna work through this."

Jason nodded and walked away without saying a word.

Chapter 36

Six months later, Jason was found not guilty for the murder of Tyrone Davis a.k.a. Tequan. He was found guilty of the murders of Henry Wright and Crystal Jefferies. The nigga and the bitch they murdered in front of Tequan's brownstone. Brian didn't know what to say, but he knew what he wanted to do. He wanted to go to that lawyer's office and get his hundred and twenty-five Gs back. Eighty was his fee, and the other forty-five was supposed to ensure that the DA would only do a half ass job. Even at half ass, he surprisingly got a conviction.

Brian sat on his couch and tried to imagine how much time the judge would sentence Jason to.

Sonia wobbled into the living room. "Get your feet off my coffee table, boy."

"Our coffee table, Boo. Come here and give Daddy some sugar." Sonia sat on his lap and gave him a kiss.

"Damn, baby. You getting heavy."

She gave him the look.

"I didn't say *fat*. I said *heavy.*"

Sonia moved to get off of him.

Brian wrapped his arms around her. "You're gonna keep me company. Talk to me."

"I got something in the oven, Brian."

"Damn, baby, you taking this wifey thing serious, huh?"

"You better start taking it serious. You got us way down here in the middle of nowhere."

"This ain't the middle of nowhere. We in ATL, baby."

Six months ago, Sonia surprised him when she came to his job at the hospital and told him that she was ready to pack her shit and move to Atlanta right now. He was shocked and happy at the same time.

A week later, he found the perfect house, with the help of his cousin, to rent with an option to buy. Sonia decided that she was going to finish her college courses online.

"Brian, come on now. I don't want the duck to burn."

"Duck? Since when I started eating duck?"

"Since tonight, if you want to eat."

Brian helped her to her feet and walked with her to the kitchen. On their way, the doorbell rang.

"Who's that?" Sonia asked.

Brian shrugged his shoulders. "I'm not expecting anybody. Go tend to your duck. I'll go see who it is."

When Brian opened the front door, his heart dropped to the center of the earth.

"Mr. Moore?" the cop asked.

"What's this all about?"

The other cop spoke. "Are you Mr. Moore?"

"Yes," Brian said. It made no sense in lying. He didn't have anything to hide.

"Mr. Moore, we need you to accompany us down to the precinct."

"For what?"

"We just need to ask you a few questions."

"You don't hear me calling you?" Sonia said, wobbling to the door. "I asked you who's at the—" Sonia's words got caught in her throat when she saw the officers at the door.

"I got to go down to the precinct for a couple minutes, baby. They need to ask me some questions."

"Why can't they just ask you right here?"

Brian looked at the officers. *Good fucking question.*

"Ma'am, we have some pictures that we will also need him to look at while he's there."

"I'm coming with you," Sonia said going to put on her shoes.

"No, baby. Stay here, finish cooking. I'll be back."

• • •

When Brian entered the station, the first thing he noticed was the New York City detectives. They stuck out like two white men at the Million Man March.

The detectives in their traditional New York manner skipped the pleasantries as they put his hands behind his back and cuffed him. "Mr. Moore, you're under arrest for the murders of Henry Wright and Crystal Jefferies."

Brian snapped. He kicked, screamed, cried, and threw himself to the ground as they struggled to get him into the car.

On their way back to New York, Brian racked his brain so hard that he thought he was going to bust a vessel. He couldn't understand how he got linked to the murders. He kept himself calm by telling himself that they didn't have any evidence against him. Devon had secured the videotape that Manny made. There were no eye witnesses to place him there, and there was no weapon. Then again, he said all of this to Jason, and they still found him guilty.

Chapter 37

When Brian entered the Brooklyn precinct, the detectives cuffed him to a table in one of the interrogation rooms. Not even a couple minutes went by before the two detectives came back in.

The chubby detective was the first to take a seat. "My name is Detective Rafferty, and this is detective—"

Brian didn't hear the other detective's name. He was preoccupied with the guns that detective Rafferty placed on the table.

He looked as if he's seen a ghost, two of them. Staring at him was the Heckler and Koch submachine gun Jason used that night, and the Beretta he used on Henry. His mind instantly took him back to the moment he was sitting in the passenger side of the stolen Lexus that night. As usual, he had given the gun to Jay to get rid of when he got rid of the truck. Only this time, Jason had kept the guns.

Did Jason give the guns up or did they search his crib and find them? Brian hoped for the latter.

Detective Rafferty interrupted his trip back down memory lane. "These look familiar to you?"

"Yeah, I see them in movies all the time."

"Wise ass, huh?" the detective said, placing a folder on the table and opening it. "You wiped the gun down. Couldn't find any prints there, but I guess wise ass ain't so wise after all. You didn't wipe down the clip."

For a moment, the scene in the room paused like a scene from the *Matrix.* Even Brian's heart was on pause.

The detective shook his head. "Then your man, your homie, your crimey came to his senses and realized that thirty to life is a long time to do in the penitentiary." He slid Jason's signed confession of what happened that night across to Brian so he could inspect it. He spilled the beans on everything, even down to where they stole the Lexus Jeep.

"It makes no sense to bullshit us. You still got a chance to make a deal and not spend the rest of your life in prison."

"Fuck you. I want a lawyer."

"Fuck you!" Rafferty said as he stood up. "And your lawyer."

Both of the detectives walked out the room, leaving him to stew in the agony of betrayal and leaving him at the hands of the annoying *tick tock* of the clock on the wall.

Chapter 38

When Sonia came to see Brian on Rikers Island, she was in shambles. Laquana had her arm around her, trying to soothe her when Brian walked out from the back.

Laquana got up and met him halfway and gave him a hug. As they walked to the table, Sonia started to get up.

"No, don't get up, baby," Brian said as he bent down and gave her a hug and a kiss. "How's our baby doing?"

"God, Brian, every day, I pray that my stress doesn't cause me to have a miscarriage," Sonia said, teary eyed.

"We're going to get through this, baby. We can't stress like this."

"I can't help it. Everything that we worked so hard for is just crumbling around us."

"I'm gonna be out of here before our little one is born. I'm gonna be in that hospital with you, helping you push that baby out, bet that." Sonia managed to put on a weak smile.

Brian looked at Quana. "What's the lawyer talk-ing about?"

"He says they ain't got nothing on you. You'll be out of here in no time."

"See, baby. I told you," Brian said to Sonia, hold-ing her hand.

Sonia looked around. "I got to go to the bath-room. I got to go like every ten minutes."

Brian helped her up.

"You want me to go with you?" Laquana asked.

"No, I'll be okay."

Brian watched her walk to the bathroom. She couldn't get there fast enough before he turned his attention back to Quana.

"What the fuck is the lawyer really saying?"

"It's not looking good, baby. He's talking about you taking a plea."

"A plea? I ain't taking no fucking plea. I want out of here. What's up with Dev?"

"Nowhere to be found."

After they picked Brian up, they went to Devon's house to pick him up as well. When his grandmother told him that detectives came by to talk to him, he didn't hang around to find out why.

Brian knew where he was though. Dev was most likely in Jamaica (the island) where most of his fam-ily resided. Before he disappeared, he brought the duffle bag of money to Quana's house and told her Brian needed her to hold on to it for him.

He gave her the money, and he held on to the drugs.

"Talk to him, Quana. There has to be something he can do, somebody I can buy off."

"I'm gonna work him."

"Jay's punk ass went up north yesterday morning," Brian spat out.

"I hope they kill his ass up there."

"Oh, don't worry. They got a crew up there called the rat hunters, and that's all they do."

"So who I got to talk to?" Quana asked.

"Nah, I'm gonna take care of it from here. You don't need to get involved with that."

"You need me to do anything?"

"All I need for you to do is stay on top of that lawyer and make sure Sonia and my kids are okay."

"Speaking of children, I saw Denise the other day. Christopher is getting big. He's walking and talking. Denise told me to tell you hi, and if you need anything, let her know."

Brian said when Sonia coming back from the bathroom, "I'm counting on you, Q. Please don't let me down."

"I got you."

Chapter 39

"**M**r. Moore," the judge said as he looked down at Brian over his glasses. "You've been found guilty by a jury of your peers. In determining the length of the sentence that I should impose on you, I took your background into consideration as well as the remorse you've shown through out the trial. I understand that you have a one-year-old son. You have a very supportive family and the letters that your friends, teachers, and employers wrote were exemplary. However, it is in the best interest of justice that I hereby sentence you to two consecutive terms of twenty-five years to life."

Everything turned black!

*The drama continues in Part 2
entitled Ol' Timer*

Part 2

Ol' Timer

Chapter 1

The morning air was crisp. Brian's nostrils flared to their maximum span, drinking it in. He hopped on the Greyhound bus, and as luck would have it, he got a window seat. For the second time in his life, he was traveling out the five boroughs. The bus ride was soothing. He took in the scenery outside of the bus as well as inside. *The ride would be perfect,* he thought to himself, *if these fucking shackles weren't biting into my flesh.*

Five days after being sentenced to two consecutive twenty-five to life sentences, he was on his way to Downstate Correctional Facility where for the next fifty years he would only be known as a number.

He closed his eyes and laid his head on the headrest. He listened to a kid who sat across from him telling the other guys what to expect when they got there. He was proud to let everybody know that this was his third time going through Downstate.

"I'm telling y'all," The kid said, "a fucking dude who used to be an inmate designed these fucking black boxes." The black box he was referring to was

257

a box that the officers placed over the handcuffs to limit the mobility of one's wrists. "And you know the fucked-up thing about it," the kid continued, "the nigga is back in jail." So I know he's kicking himself in the ass every time the officers put one of these things on him. "Serves his punk ass right."

The teen shackled to the kid didn't look a day over sixteen. His hairless face bore witness to that. He was more interested in what was going to happen at Downstate than some sell-out who invented the black box. "So what's going to happen when we get to Downstate?"

"First off, you got to understand that the CO's upstate ain't like the ones on the Island. These motherfuckers don't play. They will kill you and lose you in the system."

He went on to explain the "dehumanizing process," but Brian tuned him out. He had enough of the scared straight bullshit.

His mind went back to the courtroom. His heart started beating fast as he remembered the look on Sonia's face just before he heard her scream. Seeing her crash to the floor caused him to react without thinking. He broke free from the bailiffs in an attempt to comfort her and tell her that everything was going to be all right. They sacked him like he was a quarterback. They wrung his arms behind his back as he screamed Sonia's name over and over again. For the first time in his life, he felt powerless. From inches away, he could see her world caving in.

"Help her," he yelled to Quana who was already trying to calm her down.

Sonia leaped off the ground and pounced on the bailiffs, kicking and clawing at them. "Get the fuck off of him."

Sonia's father grabbed her by the wrists and pulled her away. "Girl, you gonna get yourself arrested."

"Don't let them take him, daddy."

Sonia sobbed in her father's chest as Brian and her father made eye contact. The disgust etched on his face sent chills through Brian. At that very moment, reality wrapped in barbed wire ripped through his mind, shredding the dreams he once had for him, Sonia, and their unborn daughter.

• • •

"Everybody, listen up," the sergeant yelled from the front of the bus. 'When you get off the bus, keep it to the right and stop at the red line painted next to the rotunda." Without waiting for confirmation, he instructed the officer to open the bus doors so that the inmates could exit.

When they got to that red line, Brian understood what it meant. As soon as they crossed it, they would belong to the state.

Just beyond the line, stood about twelve Downstate correction officers. Each one of them was built like professional wrestlers. None of them were less than six feet. Their sergeant was the only one who looked normal. He was about 5' 8" weighing in at about 160 pounds.

The sergeant from Rikers Island handed the stack of folders to the Downstate sergeant and grinned. "Have fun."

The Downstate sergeant mumbled something before sicking his goons on the fresh meat.

The inmates were huddled into a holding pen where the shackles were finally taken off. Brian could feel the blood beginning to circulate through his wrists and ankles again.

"Everybody, listen up," the Downstate sergeant said. "My name is Sergeant Sweet, but trust me, I'm far from that. From her on in, you belong to the state." He gave his words time to sink in. "Some of you, if not all of you may be retarded so let me explain what I mean. You no longer have permission to think for yourselves. You will do what we tell you to do. If you so much as fart without asking permission, I will pound you out."

At that moment, Brian finally made out the writing on the makeshift turnbuckle directly behind the sergeant. Scribbled on the black padding was "WWE Smack down." It brought a smile to his face. A smile he would soon learn would always get a nigga in trouble.

"What the fuck you smiling at?" the sergeant boomed at Brian as he walked up on him. He was so close that Brian could see the nicotine stains on his teeth. "I said what the fuck are you smiling at?"

Everyone on the goon squad flexed at the same time. Muscles jumped out at Brian from places he never knew had muscles.

"I'm not smiling at—"

Sergeant Sweet grabbed him by the neck. "You calling me a liar, motherfucker?"

Every fiber in Brian's body was telling him to knock this motherfucking crack head out. Brian out-manned him in every aspect. He would have snapped the sergeant's twig neck, but he knew he would be invoking the wrath of the goons. So he just stood there and let the sergeant choke him out. When he felt his knees buckle, he panicked and swatted the sergeant's hand from around his neck. The sergeant backed away as the wrath came. They pushed and shoved Brian between one another like lions playing with a mouse. The last thing he remembered was getting hit in the back of the head with a wrecking ball.

• • •

As Brian slept, he heard a slap way in the distance of his mind. A couple seconds later, he heard it again. This time, it was louder. The third time, it was in his ear. The fourth time, he jumped up as he felt the sting.

"He's up, boss," one of the goons said to the sergeant.

"Well, get his ass in line with the rest of them."

The goon picked Brian up by his collar and stood him up. "Walk your ass over there with the rest of them."

Brian, still stunned, squinted to see where they were. The rest of the guys he came up with were standing in front of a long table in their underwear. When Brian got to the table, the CO opened his folder. "Strip down to your underwear."

Brian did as he was told.

"Throw all that shit in that garbage bag under the table, unless you want to pay to send those clothes home."

Brian threw them in the garbage bag. No way in hell was he going to send some clothes home that he wore in jail. When he got out, he didn't want anything reminding him of prison.

From there, they all walked to a partitioned area where they were stripped frisked four at a time.

Brian was used to being stripped frisked, because it was something he had to go through after every visit on the island, but being in a POW camp in the middle of Cambodia couldn't prepare him for the Downstate reception process. He stepped into the partition with the CO.

"Take your underwear off, turn them inside out, and don't, I repeat, don't shake them."

He took them off and dropped them to the floor.

"Open your mouth wide and run your fingers through it, then lift your tongue."

Brian complied.

"Lift up your arms so I can see your underarms ... good. Now, bring your hands in front of you and turn them around... good. Now, lift your dick only... now your balls... turn around and lift up your right foot and wiggle your toes... okay. Now lift up your left foot and wiggle your toes... now bend at the waist and spread your ass cheeks wide enough for me to see up your anal cavity and don't move 'til I tell you."

Brian froze. *What the fuck? On the island, they make a nigga squat and that was it.* Brian knew from experience that niggas be trying to sneak all kinds of shit through reception. From drugs to razor blades, so he knew these motherfuckers had to be thorough, but this was ridiculous.

The CO inched up. "I ain't got all day, let's go."

To the officer, it was a job that he had become used to, but to Brian, he felt like he was about to give up his manhood. *Fuck it,* he said to himself. He knew that if he didn't do it now, they were going to beat him down, put him in the box, and make him do it another time. He bent over and blocked every-thing and everyone out.

"Okay, that's good. Put your underwear on and go stand on line."

Brian stood on the shower line, feeling violated. In his mind, he had just been raped. He wanted to just curl up into a ball in a corner somewhere and just die. When it was finally his turn to get into the shower, he had to sprinkle some powder all over his body that supposedly killed lice and shit like that, and he wasn't at all surprised that the water was frostbite cold. He stood under the thirty-second shower, wiping as much of the powder off as he could. He didn't want to be like the dude in front of him who came out with half of the shit still on him. And the sergeant didn't give a fuck. He just sent him on down the disassembly line.

After the shower, he came out and grabbed the bundle of clothes that were waiting for him on the long table. He had three pairs of underwear, two pairs of pants, two shirts, a state coat, and a pair of state boots, all courtesy of the state.

The last stop on the disassembly line was the grooming process. Everybody, unless you had a court order from the judge, had to shave all the hair off their heads and faces. Brian couldn't remember not ever having any hair on his head. He came out of his mother's womb with enough curly hair on his head to pull into a ponytail. He stared at the stranger in the mirror, and then looked at the ID numbers machine pressed on his shirt and sighed. Molested, scrubbed, shaved, and serial numbered in one day. The dehumanization process was complete.

Everyone lined up into pairs—there had to be at least fifty of them—and marched down the corridor. They stopped at each house, dumping off three to four guys from the line. Finally, they got to three complex, housing letter E. Brian and three other guys were called out and marched inside.

When Brian walked into his cell, he heard the door lock behind him. His eyes quickly focused on the mattress. Between the long bus ride and Downstate's reception process, he was dead tired. He unrolled his sheets, wrapped them around the twin-size mattress, and plopped down. He fell asleep, studying the graffiti on the walls. The last thing his eyes rested on was a cross scrawled on the ceiling right above his head with the ash from match sticks. As he sunk into a murky sleep, he wondered how many before him lay in this same position, staring at this sign of hope before closing their eyes.

As his eyes closed for the night, a tear ran down his face. He wished he could put himself in that tear, so when it evaporated he too could evaporate and be free. *There is no fucking way I'm doing fifty years of this shit,* he said. *No fucking way.*

ORDER FORM
Variety A+
P.O. Box 3807
Albany, NY 12203
_____

Name: _____

Address: _____

City, State Zip: _____

TITLES	QUANTITY/PRICES	TOTAL
Youngin'	_____ @ $15.00	$_____
Ol'Timer	_____ @ $15.00	$_____

SHIPPING/HANDLING $ 3.95
(Via U.S. Media Mail)

            TOTAL $_____

FORMS OF ACCEPTED PAYMENTS:

CREDIT CARDS
INSTITUTIONAL CHECKS
MONEY ORDERS